W9-BQZ-250

THE WHITE TOWER

THE WHITE TOWER

CATHRYN CONSTABLE

SCHOLASTIC INC. / NEW YORK

First published in the United Kingdom in 2017 by Chicken House, 2 Palmer Street, Frome, Somerset BA11 1DS.

Library of Congress Cataloging-in-Publication Data available

ISBN 978-1-338-15744-4

10 9 8 7 6 5 4 3 2 1 17 18 19 20 21

Printed in the U.S.A. 23
First edition, October 2017

Book design by Nina Goffi

C, M, R, S

I have explained the phenomena of the heavens and of our sea by the force of gravity, but I have not yet assigned a cause to gravity.

ISAAC NEWTON (1643–1727)

Rise, ye children of golde! The infinite skye awaits!

FROM *THE BOOK OF ALCHEMIE,*
PETER BURGESS (1523–1597)

CHAPTER ONE

Closing her fingers carefully around the small box in her blazer pocket, Livy craned her neck to see through the jam of bodies all shoving forward to climb onto the bus. She panicked as she saw the boy's black spiky hair disappear up the stairs to the upper deck. She had to get on this bus.

The driver looked straight ahead, uncaring. He pressed the button to close the doors. Livy pushed forward.

She was on.

The doors closed behind her and the bus lurched. Livy reached into her backpack for her bus pass. Once she had stuck it on the reader, she realized that she wouldn't be able to put it away without using both hands. She clamped it between her teeth because she didn't want to let go of that box in her pocket. This was the present—a tiny blue glass heart that she had promised her best friend Mahalia would be handed to the boy with the spiky hair—and a promise was a promise, however difficult it was to keep.

On the upper deck, Livy swung her backpack down, dropped her gym bag, and sank onto the seat. She took her bus pass out of her mouth and slipped it into her blazer pocket. The boy was sitting with his friends at the back of the bus. She took a deep breath to calm her nerves—how was she going to do this? She looked out at the clouds for help. They looked as solid as whole cities suspended above her but only made her feel more lightheaded. She would focus on letting this be a normal day, she decided. After all, what could be more normal than today?

She had gotten up when the alarm went off, as she had promised that she would: no stomachache. She had managed a whole mouthful of breakfast and gone to school. OK, school had felt a bit weird after so long, but everyone was very kind and she had sat next to Megan in math and Ciara in Spanish. That had felt wrong because she had only ever sat next to Mahalia. But she had gotten through it and here she was, going home on the bus, and the boy Mahalia was crazy about was sitting somewhere behind her. Just like normal.

Her bare knees in her summer skirt rubbed up against the seat in front of her. She wished she had worn pants but hadn't been able to find them after so many weeks off from school.

"Just a normal day," she told herself. "And tomorrow will be another normal day. And nothing much will happen. It will just be normal. Because normal is good. We like normal."

The bus's brakes screeched. She glanced over her shoulder. In the seats behind her, the boys began a round of knuckle bumping, trading friendly insults in some form of Londonish that Livy couldn't understand. Jeering laughter broke out as the boy with black spiky hair pushed his way out of the group and sauntered up the aisle toward her.

Livy took a deep breath and took the box out of her pocket.

"Excuse me?" She leaned forward.

The boy looked down at her, surprised. There was some wild whistling from his friends behind them and Livy swallowed, her throat dry. Her mind was a blank. What was she supposed to say? She thrust the tiny box wrapped in its sparkly paper at the boy's chest.

"A friend asked me to give you this," she croaked awkwardly.

"Yeah? Who's your friend?"

"You spoke to her a few times on the bus," Livy burbled.

"Is she pretty?"

Livy blushed. "She's very pretty. Long brown hair and really big eyes."

The bus stopped; Livy only had a few more seconds.

"Mahalia," Livy blurted out. "My friend is called Mahalia."

The boy took the package, held it to his ear, and shook it. "Nah," he said. "I don't know no one called Malia."

Livy took in his blazer with torn pockets, pants slung dangerously low, and his short, fat tie. His hair looked as if it had actually been glued into those strange stiff spikes. He gave her a brief shrug and headed off down the stairs.

Livy sat back in her seat. The emptiness of the day without Mahalia presented itself to her. And now this boy, who had been the focus of Mahalia's thoughts and dreams for so long, said that he didn't remember her. Couldn't even get her name right.

"Excuse me." A voice from over her shoulder.

She turned, surprised.

A slightly older boy, with curly brown hair and gray eyes, was smiling at her from the seat behind. She noticed he was wearing a pale gray blazer that did not belong to any of the local schools. On the pocket was a discreet crest of an embroidered tower. Temple College, Livy realized. The one by the river, the oldest school in London. That was where the rich children went to school; rich and clever. So what was he doing on this bus?

"Yeah?" she said, feeling annoyed.

"Is this yours?" he said, waving something in her face—then flipping it open to look at the photograph inside. "Livy Burgess."

"Where'd you get that?" Livy blurted out.

Her bus pass holder, covered in the faces of Korean pop idols that she and Mahalia adored, was in the boy's hand.

"On the floor. You dropped it."

"I couldn't have!"

"Why not?" Those large gray eyes sparkled with humor and his mouth was turned up in an impish smile. "Don't things end up on the floor when you drop them? Or do you have hidden talents?"

She swiped her hand at the card, and it dropped to the floor. They both looked down.

"Gravity." The boy shrugged. "Amazing." He scooped up the bus pass, looking at the pictures on the cover. "Are these old boyfriends?"

"They're singers!" Livy snatched the bus pass out of his hand. "Clearly!"

Livy turned back around, having given him what she hoped was a "superior" look, and took care putting her bus pass back in her blazer pocket. She pressed her cheek against the cool window, letting the city flow around her: sky like milk and the soccer stadium a cheap toy that had fallen out of a giant's Christmas stocking. Mahalia, she knew, would not have got into such a ridiculous conversation. She would have said just the thing to put the Temple College boy in his place.

She sensed him stand up behind her. "My stop," he said, as if she had asked him what he was doing. This was awkward; it was her stop, too.

She saw him out of the corner of her eye. The neat blazer on top, soccer shorts, mud-splashed legs, and filthy cleats below. He waved to her from the top of the stairs. Annoying! She waited until he had clattered down the steps and only then grabbed her backpack and hooked her finger through the string of her gym bag.

But as Livy stepped down onto the pavement, she couldn't resist looking in both directions to see which way the boy had gone. She saw him move toward the park, a long, loping stride, his head to one side as if he were listening out for something. She hung back; she didn't want to look as if she was following him, because that was her way home, too.

"Livy!"

Her mother, long black hair like trailing seaweed around her shoulders, was pushing her large old bike through the pedestrians in a determined fashion. Her eyes were made-up with their sooty black eyeliner and her lips were dark red. She looked very different from everyone else, as if she were a visitor from another country where it was normal for the inhabitants to dress in white fur coats and vintage crepe tea dresses.

"You didn't need to meet me off the bus, Mom!" Livy said, glancing around to check that no one had seen. "I'm twelve!"

"Oh!" Livy saw her mother's beautiful eyes flicker as if she'd been caught. But she quickly came up with her excuse. "I wasn't really coming to meet you." She leaned forward to kiss Livy and take the gym bag out of her hands. She smelled of roses, but roses wrapped in fur. "I needed to do some shopping!" She proudly pointed to her bike basket, which was piled high with bags of sugar and flour, a box of eggs, and several tubs of ready-made icing.

"I don't need a cake, Mom," Livy muttered. "All I've done is go to school, remember? Like everyone else."

Her mother didn't say anything as she started to push her bike toward the park. But Livy was used to these pauses where questions hung in the air and instead of speaking, her mother tried to look for the answer in Livy's face.

They walked up the side of the park; grand London terraces and stately plane trees surrounded the expanse of tired grass where dogs raced after sticks, barking recklessly. Ahead, Livy could see the boy in the pale gray blazer. Where was he going?

Her mother tried again. "It didn't feel too odd being back at school?"

Livy shook her head. She had learned over the summer that it was better just to smile an answer when the real answer was too big.

But her mother had also learned something over the last few weeks and would often know that the smile was not truthful, so Livy took the precaution of turning away.

She saw the boy in the pale gray blazer, one sock lower on his long muddy legs, stop and talk to a man standing behind a book-laden folding table. Some sort of charity fundraiser, Livy supposed. Her mother, watchful as ever, had followed Livy's gaze.

"Do you want to buy a book?" she asked hopefully. "He's got some very cheap paperbacks at his stall." She fished some coins out of her purse and handed them to Livy.

The man, thin and stooped, wore a heavy, brown three-piece suit despite the golden autumn sunshine that dripped off the trees. He had pulled a narrow-brimmed tweed hat low over his forehead. Livy began to feel anxious. She didn't want to approach the table—and the boy—and risk another conversation.

"Hi! Ros!" A woman with rainbow colors in her hair flung her hands up in delight.

"Janie!" Her mother leaned forward to kiss her friend.

Livy, too, stopped walking, relieved her mother's attention was taken so that she could watch the boy. The man bent over the table, moved some books to find what he was looking for, and handed a paperback over. The man must have said something that the boy found funny because Livy saw him throw his head back and laugh. She smiled, too, couldn't help herself.

Oh! He was going. She saw the boy wave farewell and jog-trot across the grass toward the grand terrace of Georgian houses beyond. Her mother and her fast-speaking friend were slowly walking now. Livy hung back so that she could see the boy bound up the broad stone steps of a house with a gray front door, put a key in the lock, kick open the door, and slam it shut behind him.

Livy felt herself drawn to the rickety table. She smiled shyly at the man, who smiled back, his twinkling eyes magnified by a pair of horn-rimmed spectacles. He was humming a little tune to himself and started to rearrange his piles of books. Livy wondered what book the boy had been given; the ones she could see were quite a mixture and not very interesting. There was a battered history of the Battle of Waterloo and a dog-eared French dictionary alongside a well-used thesaurus. They all looked grubby.

"Can't find what you're looking for, young lady?" The man's eyes were friendly behind the spectacles. His voice was quiet, the accent correct and precise.

Livy stepped back from the table and smiled apologetically.

"Would you like me to suggest something? I'm selling them for a good cause." The man's thin hand hovered over a large book. "What about this?" He pointed at the grinning faces of last summer's boy band.

Livy shook her head, embarrassed.

"Not your thing?" The man nodded as if he agreed with her. "What about maps? A clever girl like you should know how to read maps; it's such a bore getting lost... Or... wait a minute... I've got the one... if I can only find it... abracadabra!" He pulled out a black book with the shape of a white seagull on the cover. "This is more your thing," he said. "I can see by your face that this book will get right under your skin. He's very clever, this seagull." He tapped the book. "He learns all sorts of things as he flies through the sky."

"Oh, but—"

"Consider it a gift," the man said, smiling. "This is the book for you, I just know it. And I'll throw in this *Book of English Garden Birds.*"

"Can I at least give you something?" Livy held out the coins.

The man waved them away. "Payment enough that I have found you the right book," he said. "The right book at the right moment is medicine for the soul," he added with a look of concern.

Oh. Livy could feel her eyes prick, as if someone had blown smoke in her face. Did he know? But how could he know? She had told no one about those strange, unsettling experiences she had endured since Mahalia had gone, not even her therapist, who had asked too many questions about how Livy had felt in the weeks after it happened.

Her mother—face turned away—was still talking to her friend. Even though she was only standing a few feet away and Livy could have easily called out to her, Livy felt this was impossible. It seemed as if she was in a large glass bubble with this strange man and his books.

She stepped away from the table, clumsily stuffing the books into her backpack. She wanted to go.

"See you!" She heard her mother's voice as she said good-bye to her friend. She saw her mother turn, looking faintly startled as she saw her daughter, and start to push her bike forward.

"Well, that was all *very interesting,*" her mother said, then twittered on about somebody's husband.

Livy tried very hard to listen, but she couldn't resist looking over her shoulder, as if her head were attached to a very fine thread and it was being pulled around. The man raised his hat in an old-fashioned gesture of courtesy.

"Did you find anything interesting?" Livy's mother asked.

Livy shook her head. "It's mostly just old stuff," she muttered.

"When I walked past earlier, he tried to give me a book about an old seagull! Said he would give it to me for the price of a smile. Are you all right, Livy? You look awfully pale suddenly."

"Fine!" Livy smiled and took a deep breath. The air was dull and heavy. That was good. Anything that made her feel more earthbound was good. She closed her eyes and willed herself to be as dull and heavy as the air rather than give in to the increasingly familiar feeling that her body was weightless and could spiral up into the sky like smoke.

When your best friend dies, she thought, *everyone expects you to feel sad . . . and you do . . . but no one tells you that you might have other, more unsettling feelings that you can't talk to anyone about.*

"You're probably just tired after your first day back."

Her mother was trying not to look concerned, but Livy could see that she was biting the inside of her lip, a sign that she was worried.

"Just tired." Livy nodded.

They walked past the church, watched fraught and anxious mothers taking children into singing groups and art clubs. Twin boys in karate robes threw their squat little bodies into jumps and chops.

"Remind me to pick up Tom, will you?" Livy's mother said, more to herself than Livy. "I arranged for him to go and play at Molly's."

"So you could do your shopping?" Livy asked.

Her mother laughed, dropping all pretense. "So I could do my shopping."

She leaned her bike against the railings of their small, narrow house with the lipstick-pink front door and navy blue window frames, and got the key out of her bag.

"Mahalia's crush was on the bus," Livy said.

Her mother turned to look at her. "The one with the dreadful hair?"

Livy nodded, not trusting her voice.

Her mother shook her head. "What did she see in him?" She smiled sadly. "Mahalia was a funny, sweet girl. I know you miss her."

Rather than get into *that* conversation, Livy said, "Can I make the cake?"

Her mother looked a little surprised. "It's been a while since you made a cake," she said. "Not since before Mahalia got ill. And Dad would love it."

The door was open. Livy could see her little brother Tom's scooter, her old roller blades, and a heap of coats on the newel post. It was just like her therapist said—another normal day. Livy's mother pushed the bike up the two shallow steps, but instead of wheeling it straight into the house, she suddenly stopped on the doorstep and, speaking lightly—really, there was no emotion in her voice—said, "Dad and I wanted to talk to you about something." She pushed the bike into the hall and Livy stepped in behind her.

"What about?" Livy kept her voice neutral as she dropped her backpack on the floor and kicked it under the hall table. But the skin on the back of her neck began to prickle.

Her mother didn't say anything while she leaned the bike up against the hall radiator. She took out the bags of sugar and flour from the basket and handed them to Livy.

"You get on with the cake and I'll go and get Tom," she said, smiling. "Dad will tell you when he gets home." She flashed a smile. "Really, it'll all be fine! Nothing to worry about."

But Livy knew that whenever adults said there was nothing to worry about, there usually was.

CHAPTER TWO

"Wow!" her younger brother Tom whispered as he climbed on a chair and leaned across the kitchen table to admire Livy's handiwork. Waves of pale blue icing covered in silver balls, edible glitter, and paper butterflies risking their wings against every birthday candle in the box.

"We've got nothing to worry about, Tom," Livy said, smiling at his thoughtful face. "So I thought I'd make a nothing-to-worry-about cake!"

"Can I land this on the blue?" he said, looking up at her, a streak of dried ketchup on his chin. He uncurled his hand to show Livy his prized plastic airplane.

"Sure!" Livy laughed.

There had been days over the summer when she had felt very alone. And unlike her mother, who had looked worried or asked her how she felt, Tom had just put his arms around her and told her not to "be sad." She had spent hours lost in his flying games, and his simple adoration of her always made her feel better.

Tom lifted his arm high above his head and made whooshy noises as he made the plane come in to land. He took out a couple of candles and the wing of a paper butterfly, but looked so happy with the plane half submerged in the icing that Livy didn't have the heart to say anything.

"Now it is a boy's cake, and Dad can eat it and not die!"

The front door slammed and Tom yelled, "Dad!" and dived under the table to do his standard hide-and-pounce routine. Livy heard her parents laugh and then their voices dropped. They were no doubt discussing the "nothing to worry about." And then her father came in with his messy hair and his shirt collar peeking out of his favorite wrinkled sweater, looking as if he'd done nothing more interesting than spend all day reading on the sofa. He looked, well, normal. What was going on?

Tom leapt out from under the table, clamped his arms around his father's leg, and yelled, "Prisoner!"

His father laughed and said, "I surrender, Count Zacha!" He scooped Tom up and ruffled his hair. He looked at Livy. "Everything OK?"

He looked so hopeful that Livy made herself smile. "Yeah," she said.

"Great cake!" He collapsed into a kitchen chair, making Tom squeal with excitement as he pretended to drop him on the floor. "This is what flying feels like, hey, Tom?" He hauled Tom back onto his lap and hugged him.

Livy thought, *No, I don't think it does. I think that flying might be a lot more frightening. No one would be there to catch you.* But she didn't say anything. It was better to keep these odd, random thoughts that insisted on floating up out of nowhere to herself.

"So?" Livy's mother cut a large slice of cake and lifted it onto one of her pretty flower plates. She placed it in front of her husband.

Tom reached forward and put his finger into the wave of icing and then placed the icing in his mouth. "It tastes of blue," he said, his eyes closed.

"Hey!" Livy's father laughed. "Cake thief!"

"Don't change the subject," Livy's mother said, frowning. "You need to tell Livy your news."

Livy's dad looked at her, his expression more serious now. "Well, the news is . . . I've got a new job!" he said.

"Oh!" said Livy. This really was not much to worry about, then. "Great."

"But that's not all," Livy's mother murmured.

"I'm sure it's a very nice job," Livy said, dropping a lump of sugar into her glass of tea.

Her father looked thoughtful. "I think it is going to be a nice job," he said. "And good for all of us . . ."

"James . . ." Livy's mother warned.

Livy's father bit the corner off the slice of cake and sat forward in his chair. "Do you know Temple College?"

Livy was about to say, the school where they wear pale gray blazers? The school on the river? The oldest school in London? But her father clearly wasn't expecting her actually to answer.

"Of course you do. Well, I received a letter about a month ago inviting me to apply for the job as librarian. And I've just been appointed."

Livy glanced at her mother to gauge how she was meant to react. Was this the "nothing to worry about"?

"And the best thing is"—Livy's mother took a sip of her tea—"it means that they will offer you a place."

"If the headmistress likes you," Livy's father said, looking suddenly very serious.

"A place at Temple College?" The image of the boy's laughing gray eyes as he dropped her bus pass flared up in her mind. "But it's so expensive. Only rich kids go there."

Livy's father shook his head. "Not for you, Livy. We Burgesses may not be rich, but my job means that they will give you a scholarship so it won't cost us much. You just need to have a little interview," he said, as if this were no more challenging than eating cake.

"Interview?" Livy said. "But I can't. You know I can't."

"Why not?" her father replied.

Livy saw her mother put her hand on her father's arm as if to warn him not to press things. But this infuriated her.

"Because," she said, swallowing the lump in her throat, "because I won't know what to say to her. And I'll feel like an idiot." She pushed the plate with her slice of cake away from her. "Why don't you both stop trying to decide what's best for me and just leave me alone?"

The silence grew. She could feel that her parents were looking at each other, trying to work out how to start the conversation again. Well, she wouldn't help them. They could keep their stupid school for rich kids.

"Thing is," Livy's mother said, "Dad's new job comes with a house. We'll be moving to the school anyway. It makes sense, really, doesn't it?" There was a little gap and then her mother added, "You'll be able to roll out of bed and go straight to school! No bus, no walk, nothing. All really easy!"

"This is a fantastic chance for you, Livy." Her father's voice had a note of exasperation in it. "And for us, too. I've always wanted to work in an ancient library with a collection of rare and priceless books! Of course we'll have to leave this house and Tom will have to change his preschool, but Mom and I think it's all worth it for you to have a fresh start after what happened in the summer."

Livy felt as if she was teetering on the very edge of something and didn't know how to pull herself back.

"I just don't want to go," she said, standing up.

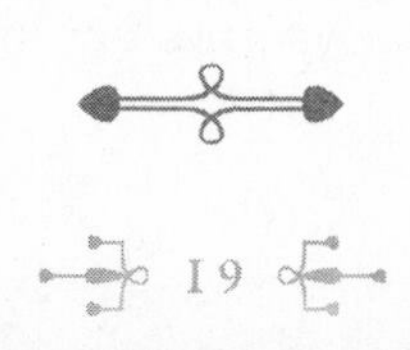

Livy lay very still in her bed. It was dark and the house was quiet. She closed her eyes. She didn't want to look into the heavy branches of the tree outside her window or watch the leaves stir in the breeze.

"Just another normal day," she said softly, as if saying those words might make it true. Like a spell. But it wasn't another normal day and she clearly had no special powers to make it that way. The day had spun out of control and images hovered in front of her eyes. The boy on the bus in the Temple College blazer. The kind man in the park and his stupid old books (which she had thrown on the floor somewhere). Her light-headedness, her shortness of breath, the "dizzy spells" that she had kept secret . . .

These had started earlier in the summer when she had visited Mahalia in the hospital and her friend could no longer do more than stare at the monitor next to her bed. Livy had pretended not to notice and tried her best to tell Mahalia what had happened at school. But it was as if she was speaking to someone very far away; Mahalia didn't respond and her parents didn't leave the bedside. Leukemia. From the Greek *leukos* and *hemia,* she had read on the Internet. White blood. When "good, normal" blood, her own blood, was red.

Livy was so upset when she got home from the hospital for the last time that she couldn't catch her breath. She couldn't seem to get the air into her lungs quickly enough.

And since Mahalia's mother had phoned with what her mother called "the saddest news," Livy had begun to have other, more worrying sensations that she couldn't tell anyone about. How could she explain how *her* blood—not white, not malignant, not *altered*—itched and pushed her up from the ground? She would look up into the large, empty sky and know in her deep, secret self that she could dive into that infinite blue as easily as she might dive in a swimming pool.

Livy pressed the backs of her legs into the mattress, trying to make herself heavy. But her body felt as if it might dissolve, like smoke.

"Livy?" Her mother's voice.

There was no point pretending to be asleep because her mother was already sitting on the side of Livy's bed.

"Why don't you want to go to Temple College?" Her mother's words hung in the air. "It's a golden opportunity for a smart girl like you."

Her parents had taken to talking to her as if she were something special, all part of their plan of making her feel more self-confident, she guessed. But it had quite the opposite effect.

If the boy in the blazer were typical of the pupils, she would struggle to make friends. He had seemed so confident, so at ease with himself, had no problem talking to people he didn't know, whereas her body was behaving so

strangely there were days when she woke up and thought that she had just been dumped in someone else's badly fitting shell.

"I'm not the right sort of girl," she whispered.

"But you can't know that," her mother said. "You have so much potential that you haven't begun to understand yet."

Livy sighed. "There's something else."

"What?"

Livy didn't want to say anything, but when her mother squeezed her arm reassuringly, she suddenly couldn't keep it in any longer.

"I promised Mahalia that we would always be friends and that no one else could ever take her place. I promised her that I wouldn't leave her." Her voice sounded a bit odd, and she really did not want to start crying. "And if she comes back to school—I know she can't, but I sometimes *have* to believe that she could—I need to be there so that she won't be alone."

Livy felt her mother's fingers on her cheek, the touch so light it was somewhere between a feather and a sigh. "Mahalia's gone too far to come back, Livy," she whispered.

Livy swallowed hard. She had spent the last difficult weeks trying so desperately not to believe this.

"And Dad and I think that you did everything possible for her. You were such a good friend."

"Perhaps I made it harder." Livy's voice was hardly more than breath, her throat dry. "Because she didn't want to leave me and make me sad."

"If we didn't care that we were leaving people we loved, what would be the point of us being here in the first place?" her mother said at last. "You have to care before you can say good-bye and mean it."

Livy closed her eyes.

"I know you feel frightened," her mother went on, "but you need to take this big step. It feels as if you're stepping into a big, empty nothing, but you've got me to hold on to you, Livy. And Dad and even little Tom, who thinks he's quite the strongest boy in the world. We'll all hold on to you."

"Promise?" Livy breathed.

"Promise," her mother whispered back. "You won't fall."

CHAPTER THREE

Livy "agreed." She would go to the "interview" with the headmistress of Temple College, Dr. Pernilla Smythe. Although she didn't really agree, she didn't seem to be able to get her parents to understand that she didn't want to go. The "interview" would have to be on a Saturday morning as Dr. Smythe was a "*very* busy woman." If, however, Livy "didn't like Temple College" despite being given this "golden opportunity," her parents "agreed" to "respect her feelings" and "think again."

"If you really *really* don't like it—" her mother said.

"Although we're confident that you will," her father interrupted.

"We won't *force* you to go," her mother added.

"Because we're not those sorts of parents." Her father smiled reassuringly. "We're *modern* parents."

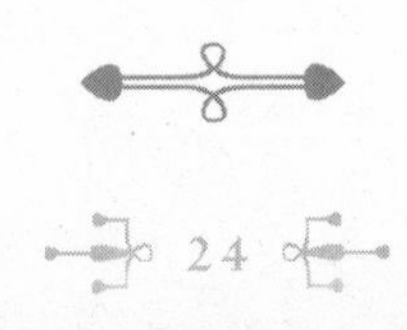

"What's an interesting view?" Tom asked, putting his plane on Livy's shoulder as her father drove them all toward Temple College.

"An interview? It's when someone looks at you and decides if you're interesting," Livy muttered. "Or not."

She felt uncomfortable; her mother had bought her a somber dress and insisted that Livy tie her hair back, take off the fingerless gloves, and swap the ankle boots for flat shoes, which almost caused a row.

"History lesson!" her father said brightly.

"Please, Dad," Livy groaned.

"Every Londoner knows Temple College!" her father announced as he swerved to avoid a cyclist. "Founded in 1563. But do they know the name of the first headmaster?"

"Um, no," Livy said. His relentless good mood was annoying.

"Who is it, James?" Livy's mother sounded genuinely interested.

"Turns out it was one Peter Burgess!"

"Hear that, Livy?" She craned around from the front seat. "Just imagine!"

"Bet he's no relation," Livy said, but the name hung in the air, insisting that it be talked about.

"He may be," Livy's father said. "I can't be sure. Maybe I can do some research in the library and find out! Dr. Smythe seems to think we're related somehow."

"Was he responsible for those statues on the roof?" Livy's mother asked, clearly choosing to ignore Livy's mood. "Those weird angels?"

"They're called Sentinels, darling. No one calls them statues or angels. And apparently Peter Burgess paid for them all. With his own gold!"

"He was rich?" Livy's mother gasped. "What went wrong? You've never had a penny!"

"Didn't need it. I'm handsome and clever!"

"Da-ad!" Livy groaned.

Minutes later, they stood on the pavement and stared up at the row of statues that lined the roof of Temple College.

"Quite something, aren't they?"

"Can they fly?" Tom's face was tipped back.

"No, darling," laughed his mother. "Of course not!"

"But they have wings!" Tom frowned. "Big ones!"

"They're made of stone, stupid," Livy muttered under her breath.

"I'm not stupid! You're a big fat stupid!" Tom cried.

"Little birds in the nest should all agree," Livy's mother said, taking Tom by the hand.

Tom shook his hand free and stuck out his tongue defiantly at Livy. She crossed her eyes and then decided to ignore him by looking up at the roof.

The Sentinels had magnificent human heads swathed

in carved curls, their expressions stern. The stone had been cut to fall in drapes, as if they were wearing long gowns. They were all different, she noticed. Some of them had their wings out and seemed to be standing on tiptoe as if they were about to take off while others had downcast heads held in prayer, their wings folded around them like cloaks.

Livy felt that they were all looking at her, waiting for her to speak.

"Look!" Tom pointed up and jumped up and down. "It's Count Zacha!"

"This is what comes of letting him watch too much television," her mother muttered. "He's obsessed with that character!"

"Why not just tell him that he doesn't exist?" Livy said.

"What?" said Tom, half hearing.

"Oh, that's right. Ruin his childhood!" Livy's mother said under her breath.

"Oh, I can see him! He's on the roof—right at the end!" Tom waved frantically at the furthest Sentinel who, unlike the others, had his back to the river and faced into Temple College. "Oh, he's gone. Will he come back?"

"Of course, Tommy," Livy said. "Count Zacha will just zoom about doing a bit of really fast flying and then he'll be right back."

Her mother glowered at her, proving that at least one other member of her family understood sarcasm.

They walked through a small arch in the bone-colored facade. They were in a sort of tunnel, with a square of daylight ahead of them. A short, round woman with gray hair scraped up into a bun stepped out of a doorway in the wall.

"Miss Lockwood," she said, putting out her hand to Livy's parents. "School secretary. Please. Come this way. Dr. Smythe is waiting for you." She looked down at Tom and sighed. "Oh dear. Perhaps we should hide the small *thing*. Dr. Smythe is not keen on"—she waved her hand at Tom as if she could shoo him away—"miniatures."

"I'll keep hold of him," Livy's mother said, catching Tom's hand.

Miss Lockwood looked uncertain but ushered them through the arch and into a courtyard.

They were now surrounded on all sides by walls of gray stone and rows of blank windows. There were plain stone arches and recessed doorways at regular intervals. Everything was ordered, precise, and architecturally consistent. Except in one corner was a narrow, pale tower of flint and brick, much older-looking than the rest of the buildings. The parapet around the roof had weeds growing out of the stone, and all of the windows were bricked up, apart from one, near the top. That small, blank window gave the tower a desolate air. The iron-studded door at the bottom was closed.

It was on the roof of this tower that the farthest Sentinel stood. With its carved face lifted to the sky, it looked as if it could step into the air at any moment. Livy held her breath as she imagined the Sentinel reaching up to the clouds and shaking out those enormous wings before leaping into the air and flying powerfully upward, free at last from centuries of standing on the roof of Temple College. But then she saw that one of its wings was broken. If the Sentinel were to move, it could only fall, landing in pieces on the flagstones below.

Livy shuddered at the image of the falling Sentinel. She felt suddenly that she wanted to run back to the car. She had pins and needles in her fingers and she could feel her heels rising up off the flagstones. She tried to breathe, to make herself feel as heavy as the Sentinels. *Normal is good,* she told herself, but then, since Mahalia had died, she had less confidence in what was *normal.*

Standing in the center of the courtyard was a woman with bright gold hair. She walked quickly toward them in very high heels and a beautifully tailored gray suit. The headmistress, of course.

Livy sighed as she thought of the impression she would make in her unflattering new dress with its droopy hem and high collar. Her mother had called it "charmingly

Victorian with a touch of Gothic drama." Livy called it ugly.

Livy's father said, "Dr. Smythe! Here we are! Thank you so much for seeing us."

"They've brought an extra," Miss Lockwood whispered under her breath. "What should we do?"

Dr. Smythe's chiseled face barely softened as she looked down at Tom. "And who are you?" she asked.

"This is Tom," Livy's father said.

"Tom!" Dr. Smythe said, as if she had never heard such an interesting sound.

"I can fly!" Tom said brazenly.

Dr. Smythe blinked in surprise, but spoke to Tom quite seriously. "The founder of Temple College, Peter Burgess, would have been interested to know how you do that, Tom. He spent most of his life trying to understand gravity." She raised an eyebrow at Livy's father. "Quite the golden boy, James."

Tom stared up at the woman, entranced. "Do you know Count Zacha?"

Dr. Smythe frowned. "I'm not sure I do, Tom. Would you draw a picture of him for me?"

"Well," Miss Lockwood looked surprised, "he's a charmer!"

Livy wondered if she would be so successful at charming Dr. Smythe. Thinking of the hours of interview preparation her father had given her, she thought it would take more than boasting that she could fly and drawing a picture of Count Zacha.

Dr. Smythe addressed her parents. "My secretary will give you coffee while I have a chat with Livy."

"I was hoping to take another look at the library," Livy's father said. "I'm itching to get back in there." He rubbed his hands together. "Especially the really old books that belonged to Peter Burgess. I can't wait to see what you have!"

"Even better!" Dr. Smythe smiled.

She turned toward a doorway on the far side of the courtyard. "Come along, Livy, this won't take long."

CHAPTER FOUR

Livy fixed her eyes on Dr. Smythe's heels, which were as high and sharp as hypodermic needles. Her father had explained that Pernilla Smythe was a scientist of the highest order. She had, apparently, won awards, written papers on gravity, run laboratories in Prague, all while looking for things called "superheavy elements." Educated at Temple College, she had recently returned as its headmistress, drawn back by the wealth of material in the school's extensive and priceless library. She wanted to see if any of the Temple scholars' work from centuries ago might be of interest to her. "So my job as librarian will be very important," Livy's father had said. But his description of the headmistress had made Livy imagine a much older woman with frizzy gray hair and frumpy clothes, whereas Pernilla Smythe, in the flesh, was impossibly glamorous. How could Livy impress her? She had only just started studying the periodic table before all that time off from school, and what she'd learned she had forgotten.

Dr. Smythe disappeared through an archway next to the narrow tower. Pushing through the door after her, Livy saw the woman climbing an enormous stone staircase at some speed.

Livy climbed the stairs after her, two at a time, trying to catch up; she was briefly aware of the framed certificates that hung on the wall. They were in all sorts of languages, with letters picked out in gold. But they all had two words in common: Pernilla Smythe.

A door had been left open at the top of the stairs and Livy stood in the doorway, looking into a large book-lined study. She wasn't sure what she should do.

"Come in!" Dr. Smythe waved Livy forward.

Stepping into the room, Livy saw a window that took up the full height of the wall from the ceiling to the floor and seemed to have been placed there purely to frame the Sentinel with the broken wing standing on the top of that strange, out-of-place tower.

"Come farther in!" Dr. Smythe called. "I can't speak to you from there."

Livy closed the door behind her and walked reluctantly toward the woman who was now seated behind an enormous mahogany desk covered in very neat stacks of papers.

"Ouch!" Livy caught her leg on something and heard the crack of glass. Looking down, she saw that she had walked into a corner of a large packing crate in which several glass flasks were lying on piles of golden straw. "I'm so sorry!"

"Don't worry," Dr. Smythe said from behind her desk. "You're not hurt?"

Livy shook her head although her shin had been begun to throb.

"Let's hope that nothing is broken. That box contains equipment for my laboratory," the headmistress murmured. With a wave of her hand, she indicated that Livy should take the seat opposite her. On her wrist was a large gold charm bracelet that looked too heavy for the woman's delicate bones. "Flasks of that quality are very hard to get in this country—I had to have those sent over from Prague. I am about to resume my research into an obscure theory of gravity and I am certain that your father is going to be a great help in finding some scientific books that have gotten lost in the depths of the library."

Livy sank into her seat, silently relieved that by the time Dr. Smythe discovered the broken flask, Livy would already be out of the room.

"Are you sure you're not hurt?" Dr. Smythe asked, though she sounded impatient. "You look pale."

Livy shook her head again. In truth, she didn't care

about the painful shin. What she was having trouble with was the sky . . . Being this high up in a room with such a huge window made her feel light-headed. Perhaps if she just stared at Dr. Smythe, away from all the sky, away from the Sentinel, she could lock herself in her body. But the window had been left partly open and she could feel a draft around her neck, could smell the clouds, and hear the flap of a pigeon's wings.

"Livy?"

"Yes?" Her voice was too loud.

Dr. Smythe had followed her gaze, her eyes as sharp as her heels. "I have days when I quite expect the Sentinels to speak," she said slowly. "They're so lifelike, aren't they?"

Why isn't she talking about chemistry? Livy thought. Or physics? She sighed and twisted around so that she couldn't see the window at all. She thought, *The Sentinels would be more likely to fly than speak.*

But to her horror, she saw by the startled expression on Dr. Smythe's face that she hadn't thought those words, she had spoken them. Out loud. She dug her nails into her palms and the pain made her feel braver. Oh, what did it matter what Dr. Smythe thought of her?

But the headmistress looked thoughtful. "What an interesting thing to say," she said. "Did you know that there were some scholars at Temple College who believed that they had the power to make the Sentinels move? Even to fly like angels. But they had very different ideas about what science could do and what science was for back then. All very foolish, of course."

Livy shook her head in confusion. "But no one could make a stone statue move. That's ridiculous!"

"You might be surprised, Livy, by what scientists think."

Behind the desk hung a large, dark oil painting of a man with a pale face, wearing black scholars' robes. He looked as if he was peering through a haze of smoke to find out what Livy might say next. In the painted sky above his head hung both the sun and the moon. He held an hourglass in his thin white fingers. The man must have just turned it over because the sand had not reached the bottom of the globe. And along the bottom of this perplexing portrait, Livy saw two words: *Tempus Fugit.*

Dr. Smythe turned to the painting. "Take Peter Burgess," she explained. "The first headmaster of Temple College when it was founded in 1563. A superb scientist. And one of your ancestors!"

"Dad said we *might* be related," Livy said, looking at the dark, heavy-lidded eyes that bore no resemblance to her own hazel ones. "But I'm not sure I believe it. We're quite poor and Dad said that Peter Burgess had loads of money."

Dr. Smythe smiled thinly. "He had lots of gold, it's

true," she said. "He became fabulously rich almost overnight, although he never said where the gold came from. And he used the gold that he acquired to do some good in the world. He collected rare and precious books that gave Temple College an unrivaled library. He plucked six poor boys from the parishes of London and educated them at his own expense. He called them his scholars. You can see their names on a board outside the Temple that gives the school its name. And, just before he withdrew to the White Tower where he lived out the rest of his life as a recluse, he paid for all seven Sentinels that guard Temple College to be carved by a master stonemason." She frowned. "Odd that he ordered seven Sentinels when there were only six boys. But perhaps it was cheaper to carve a statue than educate a child." Her eyes glittered with interest. "Master Burgess fascinates me. While I was working in Prague, I found out quite a lot about the mysterious Peter Burgess. Like so many scholars of the time, his scientific work was all bound up in his religious beliefs. He thought that gravity was brought into the world when Adam and Eve were banished from the Garden of Eden for eating from the Tree of Knowledge. This sinful act, he believed, made their blood heavy and they fell to earth. Peter Burgess thought that, before that fall, humans were immortal and could fly like angels."

Livy pressed her heels down into the floor as her

own blood surged upward in her veins. The work of Master Burgess did not sound very scientific and yet Dr. Smythe's words were having a strange effect on her body.

"Peter Burgess was born almost a hundred years before Isaac Newton, who we know discovered gravity, and yet here he wrote about why objects fell to the ground through an invisible mortal force. If only so much of his work had not been lost! I hope that your father will help me find the notes to his last experiment." Dr. Smythe sighed. "The records in the library have not been well kept."

Livy looked at the dark painting. Could that man with his strange and very unscientific ideas that so interested Dr. Smythe really be some distant relation of hers?

"Just think," Dr. Smythe said quietly. "You might have the blood of the great Peter Burgess flowing through your veins . . ."

Livy stared at her hands and the blue veins that showed through her white skin. "Whether I'm related to Peter Burgess or not, it doesn't make any difference to what's in my veins," she said, thinking of Mahalia and how her doctors had hoped to transform her blood with their powerful chemicals. "I'm sure it is the same as anyone else's." She flexed her fingers to get rid of the pricking sensation in them.

"Perhaps," Dr. Smythe said, looking at Livy steadily. She flicked through some papers on her desk. "You've missed a lot of school recently."

Livy looked at her shoes. "My friend—" she started to say, but Dr. Smythe interrupted her.

"However, although your academic record is patchy, due to your having been absent for almost a term of your present school, still, I think there is every reason to believe that the scholarship place that comes with your father's new job will not be wasted on you. I will make a formal offer of a place to your parents."

Dr. Smythe stood and held out her hand.

Livy stood, too, and shook the offered hand, which was as cool and smooth as polished metal.

"Is that all?" she asked, surprised at being dismissed. "Is the interview over?"

Dr. Smythe nodded, with a faint smile. "I think that Peter Burgess would approve of your being a scholar here," was all she said.

"Perhaps," Livy repeated, looking up at the painting. Why were the moon and the sun in the same sky?

"Just one more thing before you go." Dr. Smythe was already sitting back down and looking at her papers. "Your brother, Tom. How old is he?"

"Tom?" Livy asked, puzzled. "He's four."

Dr. Smythe bent her head and wrote something quickly on her papers. As she did not raise her head again, Livy turned and left the office.

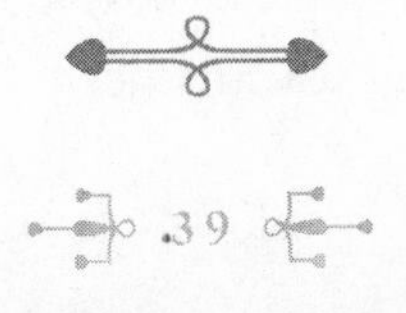

Livy walked slowly down the stairs, past all Pernilla Smythe's certificates and degrees. She felt suddenly deflated. Her father had prepared her for being asked about her studies and what subjects she enjoyed, but Dr. Smythe had not been interested. And yet Livy had been handed a place just like that. Was it really enough to be distantly related to Peter Burgess?

She stepped out into the courtyard; her parents were nowhere to be seen.

She stood at the edge of a puddle, looking at the reflection of the sky. She inched forward so that the reflected angel's wings appeared to come from her own shoulders. But what was that? Hovering just between "her" wings? A twisting black shape made of smoke or shadow . . . Startled, she looked up. No—there was nothing but the Sentinel, staring at the clouds, and a bird wheeling around the beautiful carved stone head.

"What do you think?" she said to the Sentinel. "Should I come here?"

But the person whose opinion she really wanted was Mahalia. *What would she say?* Livy wondered then. If only she could find a way to talk to her friend, to tell her where she was, to ask what she thought . . .

"Livy!"

She turned to see her parents walking quickly across the courtyard and Tom twisting his hand out of his mother's and running toward her.

"How did it go?" her father asked.

Her mother was looking at her hopefully. Livy knew that Tom had already been enrolled in his new preschool, that her father had bought a new suit for "the job of his dreams," and that her mother had started packing up their house and booked the moving van. Livy starting at Temple College was just the last piece in the puzzle that would be their new life. How could she tell them that she was unsure?

But then, life was about to change whether she wanted it to or not.

She shrugged. "Dr. Smythe is not *awful,* I suppose." Livy felt that she had no choice but to be resigned to her fate.

Her father squeezed her shoulder. "That's the spirit! Let's go and see the new house. You can choose your bedroom!"

CHAPTER FIVE

To get to the librarian's house they had to walk out of Temple College and turn into a small side street of tall, thin houses that backed onto the school walls. LEADEN LANE, Livy read on an old-fashioned metal street sign fixed to the side of the first house.

"We're number seven!" Livy's father announced, drawing a large bunch of keys out of his pocket. "This house is very old, Tom," he said, looking up at the dark brick facade. "Can you guess how old it is?"

"Forty-three?" Tom offered.

"It was built in 1720. That's nearly three hundred years old!"

Tom shut his eyes tight. "Don't like!"

As her father pushed open the dark gray front door, Livy's mother wrinkled her nose. "It needs a good airing."

Large packing crates blocked their way. "Didn't the last librarian take his things with him when he moved?" Livy's mother asked, looking worried. "I thought you said everything would be ready for us when we moved in."

Livy's father kicked some crumpled newspaper to one side as they stepped over a pile of letters into the dark, narrow, paneled hallway.

"Oh, James," Livy's mother said. "I'm not sure about this."

"We can paint the walls brighter colors," Livy's father said breezily. "We don't have to keep everything this drab gray."

"If you say so." Livy's mother picked up Tom, but she didn't sound very sure.

Livy's father opened a door and they all peered into a small, dank sitting room. "Let's not be disheartened," he said as they all felt just that.

"But, James!" Livy's mother sighed.

"Not a word until we've had a good look around!"

Livy chose the room next to Tom's; it was slightly larger and had a view over the wall to the Temple College gardens. But as they were about to go back downstairs—her father squeezing her mother's hand and whispering,

"Will it do? It's not very big but it's got plenty of character, shutters in every room and all the fireplaces work"—Livy saw a narrow door.

"Can we have a look in there?"

Her mother sneezed. "I think I've had enough dust for one day. Can it wait?"

But Livy was overcome with curiosity. She could feel a slight breeze coming from behind the little door. She turned the handle and the door swung open to reveal a steep staircase going up.

She could hear Tom asking for his new toy plane, bought the day before, and her mother's exasperated voice: "Hang on!"

Livy ran up the stairs.

She was in a small room; the roof came right down to the floor on two sides. If she put her arms out, she could nearly touch the walls. There was an odd smell, too. Bitter and metallic.

The window, which jutted out into the sky so that if you stood in the little box of the frame, you could see to the right and the left, was open. A piece of red thread had gotten caught on the window frame and it fluttered in the breeze.

She heard footsteps on the stairs. "It looks like a maid's room," Livy's mother said, arriving out of breath. "It probably once belonged to a girl the same age as you, employed to clean all the fireplaces and light the fires."

"Can I have this room?"

"But it's too small!"

"I don't mind!"

"But why do you want to be up here?"

Livy looked out at the sky and the Sentinel that she could see through the window. She wasn't sure why she wanted to be up here, but it felt as if the room—that view—had been waiting for her.

"You'd have to cope with the furniture that's in here because we wouldn't be able to get anything else up those stairs. And it's right up in the roof! You'll be frozen in winter and boiling in summer."

"I don't care!" Livy said. She stroked the fading wallpaper of ivy and roses trailing over a stone wall. It was like being inside a tower. She took in the chipped paintwork and the laundry line strung across the boarded ceiling. She sat down on the narrow iron-framed bedframe. Mahalia would like this room, Livy decided. It would be good for epic chats.

Her mother, answering her father's call, went quickly down the stairs again.

Livy was alone.

The silence settled around her. She allowed herself to fall back onto the soft and rather lumpy mattress, which was covered in a faded flower print. Her stomach turned as she fell.

She put both hands behind her head and looked at

the window full of sky, the clouds as thin and white as smoke. From this angle, she could see only one Sentinel—of course, she thought, the one who guarded the pale, derelict tower in the courtyard. Its face was turned away as if it had just heard something and its whole being seemed alert, as if it might take off. But no, Livy thought. That was just silly. How could a block of stone fly, however lifelike?

It was hard to tell what sex the creature was, Livy thought, with those long curls and strange flowing robes. She wasn't meant to call it an angel, her father had said, but if any creature were to fly through the infinite sky, surely it would look like this. Perhaps the Sentinel could take off and fly toward wherever Mahalia was. That thought warmed her. She hated to think of Mahalia in a cold, dark, distant and silent place with no one to talk to. She and Mahalia had loved to talk—spent all their time talking. If this creature could only reach her and let her know . . . let her know that Livy had not forgotten her. Was still talking to her—or trying to. If only Mahalia would answer.

As she stared at the wings, she saw—she was sure of it!—one of the great stone feathers tremble in the breeze.

Livy gasped.

The feather shivered again.

She continued to stare at the stone but forced herself to think sensibly.

"I am Livy Burgess," she said to the Sentinel. "And you are a statue. There is no way that the feathers in your wings can move."

Livy relaxed her gaze. Now the feather was still.

"Stone is stone," she whispered. "And blood is just blood, whoever you're related to."

Though that hadn't been true for Mahalia—her blood had altered into a poison that had destroyed her.

"Liveeeeeeee!" Tom's voice filled her head as he clomped noisily up the stairs. "I got Count Zacha's Warrior Copter!"

She turned her head as her brother shot into the room bringing a riot of colorful plastic right up to her eyes. She smiled weakly at his bright little face—so alive—his plump fingers clutching the toy . . .

"It can fly!" he cried out in excitement. "It has swords and wings! Get up!" Tom pulled at her arm. "Get up or I will fire at your head with Count Zacha's Venom Blade!"

CHAPTER SIX

The night before she started at Temple College, Livy laid out her new school uniform on the table in her new bedroom. The pale gray woolen blazer with its embroidered tower on the breast pocket had been so ruinously expensive that her mother had gasped as she handed over her credit card to pay for it. She had insisted on buying her one that was too big to give Livy plenty of room to grow into; Livy was going to look ridiculous.

She lay in bed. It was already late and she had been told to get a good night's sleep, but how could she sleep? She was too wound up even to close her eyes.

On the shelf above the desk were her tiny stack of toy animal erasers, the stone she had painted to look like a mouse, and the snow globe with the tiny castle on the hill that Mahalia had given her for her tenth birthday. Her books were in a little bookcase and the posters of the Korean pop stars had been put up (*not her old boyfriends,* she said to herself, remembering the boy on the bus). Her mother had hooked up curtains made of glittering sari silk—they fell over the small window like a sparkling waterfall.

She picked up an old matchbox that had been tucked behind the snow globe. She hadn't opened it, hadn't dared open it since the day she had been told that she wouldn't see Mahalia again. Taking a deep breath, she slid the box open and tipped the disc of dirty brown metal into her hand. Three feathers above a crown and the words TWO PENCE around the edge.

"What do you want to keep this for?" her mother had laughed as she had bustled in to pack up Livy's room for the move. But seeing Livy's face she had put it back in its place. "Why don't you put the things that are important to you in the same box so that they don't get lost?"

Staring down at the coin, Livy could see Mahalia laughing as she had picked it up from the ground. "It's my lucky penny," she'd said, looking at the back of the person who had dropped it. "And look, it's a two pence piece, so I get double the luck!" But Livy had thought she had said, "I get lubble the duck" and they had laughed about it all the way to the bus stop.

She sank down on the edge of her bed, still staring at the coin. So much had changed in the last few weeks and now it was going to change again.

"It's no good," she thought out loud. "I've made a mistake. I'll never fit in down there."

As the words hung in front of her, she heard a faint tapping noise.

It was like a bird's beak against the window, but there was no bird on the windowsill. There it was again, but it sounded more like a teaspoon against a glass.

"Mahalia?" she whispered. Just to say her name out loud gave her a thrill.

She got up and went to look out the window.

Just the sky, the clouds, and the Sentinel. A twist of gray smoke rising up from the roof of Temple College. But nothing that could have made a tapping noise. No Mahalia. Of course. How could it be otherwise? Mahalia was somewhere else.

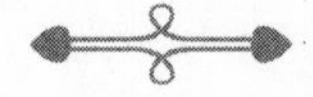

She was woken the next morning by the sound of her mother's voice calling up to her to get a move on and brush her teeth. Her head felt heavy; she had gone to sleep so late and was now exhausted. She dragged her uniform on and stumbled down the stairs to the kitchen.

"All ready for your first day?" Livy's father smiled at her as he stood next to the kitchen sink drinking his coffee.

Livy shrugged. "As ready as I'll ever be starting at a school I'll never fit into."

"Livy!" Her mother looked surprised. "What do you mean? We talked about this and you said that you were happy to go to Temple College."

Livy sighed. What was the point? Her memory was that her parents had talked to her about starting at Temple College and what a good idea it was, and that she had said very little.

"Shall I walk you over?" her father said. "So that you don't have to go in alone?"

"You want me to turn up at a new school with my dad?" Livy said. She could feel her cheeks flaring. "Isn't it enough that I look ridiculous in this stupid blazer?"

Livy saw her mother frown slightly and turn away. "I think you look very nice in your blazer," she said.

"Just be yourself," Livy's father told her.

Livy groaned and left, banging the door behind her.

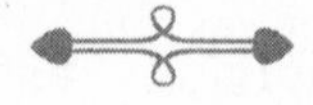

Only a few minutes later, she stood awkwardly in the small guard building just outside the entrance to the main courtyard. Someone was bound to come and find her if she waited here. Her brand-new blazer was too heavy and as stiff as cardboard. Her new school pants itched. Her

heart was pounding. She couldn't leave; she had to get through this day somehow. And without a friend. "Just be yourself," her father had told her, as if this was some magic formula that would bring her happiness and friendship. But who was she? Livy was less and less sure of herself since Mahalia had died.

"Excuse me," Livy said to the security guard who sat behind the desk. The man took no notice of her as he drank tea and stared at a small monitor flicking through grainy black-and-white images of various parts of the school, all unknown to her.

"Are *you* Olivia Burgess?"

Livy had been so intent on watching the monitor that she hadn't noticed a tall girl carrying a pile of three-ring binders enter the room.

"Yes, but people call me Li—" she started to say.

The girl spoke across her. "I'm Samira. Mr. Bowen sent me to find you."

"Mr. Bowen?"

"Housemaster of Burgess. That's your house. Where you have your locker and go for registration. All the houses at Temple College are named after famous scientists who were educated here. I suppose someone thought it was funny to put you in Burgess. I'm in Maskelyne. He was a famous astronomer." She clicked her fingers and turned on her heel. "Quick, quick," she said. "There isn't much time."

A bell rang, a deep clang that made Livy's rib cage quiver. The noise poured over them as they stepped into the courtyard.

"This is called the Court of Sentinels," the girl explained. "No prizes for guessing why." She raised her eyebrows to the roof.

Livy had the powerful sensation that she wanted to be up on the roof and away from the anxiety of the day. Up there, she felt, she could rest her head on a cloud, stretch out as if she were still in bed and, somehow, if she concentrated hard enough to hold on to her voice, talk to Mahalia.

In the courtyard, groups of students in blazers just like hers stood around in small groups or walked briskly toward various doorways. They all seemed to be talking animatedly to one another, backpacks on shoulders or dropped to the floor. Brimming with all these voices and movement, Temple College seemed very different from the empty place that she had walked through with Dr. Smythe. A soccer ball rolled in front of the girl with the files and, without breaking her pace, she kicked it, hard, back to the group of boys, who shouted their thanks.

"See that door?" The girl pointed to the corner of the courtyard. "Go in there. You need the first door on the right."

Samira moved away but turned back to say, "Someone will see you. Probably."

Livy stood awkwardly outside the "first door on the right." It was open, but Livy didn't think she should go in. A small, thin girl with wide cheekbones and large violet eyes appeared at Livy's side and observed her from beneath heavy black bangs.

"You have to knock on the door," the girl said. "Mr. Bowen's always busy so he won't notice you."

"Thanks," Livy said.

She knocked on the door. Nothing happened. The girl reached out and gave the door two smart knocks.

"That should do it." She turned to study the notice board.

"Yes!" A voice cried out. "Don't hang around out there! Come in!"

Livy took a deep breath and stepped into a cluttered office. A bald man wearing heavy round glasses sat behind a desk covered in exercise books and papers. "What is it?" he said, not looking up from covering a page in red ticks.

"I'm . . . I'm . . ."

The man glanced up and put down his pen. "Oh!" he said, smiling. "You're Livy! I completely forgot that you were starting today." He pushed his chair back and cried out, "Celia? Can you get in here?" He took off his glasses and blinked at her. "I must say it's very nice to welcome an

actual Burgess to Temple College finally, after, what is it? Almost five hundred years! Where did Dr. Smythe find you?"

Livy shrugged.

Mr. Bowen looked thoughtful and added, "A living, breathing Burgess!"

There was a knock on the door. "Ah! Celia," he said. "I didn't think you would take so long to appear considering that I saw you outside only a second ago."

The girl who had been standing by the notice board looked at Livy with interest.

"This is Livy Burgess," Mr. Bowen said. "It's her first day at Temple College."

"Is this the new librarian's daughter?" Celia said. "The one who hasn't had to do the entrance exam?" She put her hand over her mouth.

"How do *you* know that?" Mr. Bowen shook his head. "Well, never mind—it would be a great help, Celia, if you could show her how to register and where her locker is; make Livy feel really welcome at Temple College."

Once outside, Celia was about to speak when she was interrupted by two girls who ran up to her, out of breath.

"We've seen him, Celia," said one, a tall girl with long brown hair pulled into a ponytail on the side. Her skirt was short, she wore her socks pulled over her knees, and her lips were suspiciously red and glossy. She had a large

handbag over her shoulder and was holding out her phone—the latest model, Livy noticed—to show Celia the screen. "See? I filmed him!"

"Joe?" Celia squealed with excitement, snatching at the phone. "Joe Molyns?"

"See how fast he's running?" said the other girl. She had a sharply cut blond bob and pale blue eyes, with very long, very black lashes. Her skirt was also rather short and her blazer seemed too tight. Mahalia would have called her a "shiny girl" and kept away. "He was really late for something. Who's this?"

"This is Livy," Celia said quickly. "New girl." She craned her neck to see through the door into the courtyard beyond.

"I can see that!" the blond girl said. "Didn't they have a blazer in her size?" She gave a little snort.

"Livy looks extremely put together, Amy," Celia said. "Not everyone customizes their school uniform like you!"

"But pants!" The girl with the brown ponytail made a face.

"Martha. Don't be mean!" Celia said. "She can't know everything on day one!" All Livy had thought was that she and Mahalia preferred pants. Celia pulled Livy down the corridor, Amy and Martha following close behind. "Come on, we've got to get your fingerprints scanned."

"Why?" asked Livy, alarmed.

"That's how we register at Temple College," Celia said.

"And we're not going to take long," Amy said. "Because if we hurry, we can still catch Joe Molyns."

CHAPTER SEVEN

The four girls dropped their bags in the locker room, scanned Livy's fingerprints, and set off across the Court of Sentinels.

"I can't see him." Celia turned her head from side to side, disappointed. "Maybe he's in the Temple already?"

"We would have caught up with him if we hadn't had to spend so long getting registered," Amy muttered.

Livy was going to say something, but remembered how Mahalia would always tell her to keep quiet when the shiny girls started. "They just want the attention," she would whisper as she pulled Livy away from a possible incident. "Don't give them what they want."

Celia, walking in front with Livy, took no notice. "What school were you at before?" she asked.

Livy told her.

Celia shook her head. "Never heard of it."

"It's not well-known like Temple College."

"Did you like it?" Celia asked.

Livy looked up to see the girl's bright, curious eyes regarding her. She thought about the squeaky floors, leaking windows, and drafty corridors.

"It was all right," Livy said, and then felt annoyed with herself for replying in such a boring manner.

"Well, school is school," Celia shrugged.

"Unless you're at Temple College!" Amy interrupted. "My parents wouldn't let me go anywhere else! And, of course, I passed *all* the entrance exams for *all* the top London schools so I could choose where to go."

Celia asked, "Will you miss your friends?"

Livy nodded and muttered, "I suppose."

"Who will you miss the most?" Celia leaned in as if Livy was about to tell her a great secret.

Livy swallowed. Her throat felt as if she had a huge glass marble stuck in it. "My best friend. But she moved away," she whispered. "At the beginning of the summer. So I don't really see her anymore."

"I can't understand anything she says!" she heard Martha whisper behind her. "Her accent!"

"And look at that bag she's carrying. It's a backpack! Urgh!"

But when Livy turned around, both girls smiled at her.

"Just saying we *love* your bag," Amy said. "So rustic!"

"Did you know that Livy's dad is the new librarian?" Celia said. "That makes her nearly a celebrity."

"He's on the *staff*?" Amy said, horrified. "Are you on a *scholarship*?"

Livy shrugged.

"That hardly matters, Amy," Celia said. "It's just fascinating that Livy's father is the new librarian. Especially after the last one left so suddenly!" She leaned in close again. "Dr. Smythe sacked him! Let's hope nothing like that happens to your dad."

They had entered a cloister; a covered path led them around a square of emerald green grass toward a vast door.

"Does everyone like Dr. Smythe?" Livy asked.

"Total buzzkill," Celia sighed, then brightened. "Mr. Bowen said that you are an actual Burgess!" She turned to Livy as if she might be able to tell if it were true or not from merely looking at her face.

"It's my name," Livy replied. "But I'm not sure that it means very much."

"But you're related to Master Burgess? The first headmaster of Temple College? You have a Temple College house named after you!"

Livy shrugged. "Dr. Smythe seems to think so."

"And now you turn up." Martha snapped her fingers. "Just like *that*."

"You must have taken an exam," Amy said. "My parents say that everyone has to take an exam. Temple College doesn't let just *anyone* in!"

"But if she's related to Peter Burgess . . ." Celia whispered.

Livy couldn't think what to say. But now they were in the crush of bodies lining up to get into the vast door—the temple after which the school was named, Livy assumed. Celia was explaining that it was not built for religious reasons, but as a meeting place for the scholars who had founded the school to debate with one another and present scientific papers. It looked more like a cathedral, Livy thought, with its flying buttresses and stained-glass windows. It was certainly grander than any part of her last school, where all assemblies had been canceled since the sports hall flooded five years ago.

"Just so that you know," Celia was saying, "Temple assembly is really boring. Dr. Smythe will just rattle on, but don't fidget or you'll get one of her death stares and wind up in one of her weird detentions where you have to clean out all the dirty flasks from the chemistry lab."

A riot of bells broke out over Livy's head.

"Oh, and put your phone on silent," Celia hissed.

Livy did it but knew no one would be likely to text her. She currently had no friends.

The bells changed to a single, repeated chime. There was a surge of bodies from behind and a man's voice intoned, "All Templars will be seated."

Celia pushed her into a row of chairs near the back and Livy looked up into the crystal petals of a chandelier that hung from the high, vaulted stone ceiling.

A boy with ragged blond hair, so thin that the collar on his shirt was too big, appeared at the end of the row. "Can you move along, please?" he said to Livy. "The teachers are about to come in."

"No, Alex." Amy leaned forward and made a shooing gesture with her hand. "No room for you here."

"Amy!" the boy pleaded and then he looked at Livy. "Can't you move over?"

At that moment, teachers began to file in from a side entrance, all wearing long academic gowns. The boy said something under his breath and darted off to find another seat.

"Good riddance," Amy said, smiling at Livy. "We can't have *him* hanging around."

But Livy felt sorry for the boy. She should have forced the others to move over for him.

As the teachers took their place in the Temple, it felt to Livy as if she was watching a play. No teacher at her last school had worn a black gown, there had been no processions, and certainly no ancient bells ringing out overhead. She had a strange sense of being not only in the wrong place, but in the wrong time, as well. Surely no one behaved like this in the modern world?

There was a scraping of chairs and coughing as all the pupils stood up; Livy quickly followed suit. At the end of the procession of teachers, Livy saw Dr. Smythe, her shoulder-length hair falling in solid golden waves. The general background noise of voices immediately dropped away as the woman walked past on her way to the raised platform at the front of the Temple. The rest of the teachers remained standing until Dr. Smythe had taken her place on a large carved wooden chair.

"Scoot over!" she heard a boy's voice say. "Quick, otherwise I'll have to sit on the floor!"

Livy looked up, then felt a sharp tug on her arm and turned to see Celia, her cheeks flaming.

"It's Joe Molyns!" she whispered, pulling Livy down one chair so that the boy could sit down. Martha and Amy started whispering together excitedly.

The boy seemed oblivious to the girls' twittering and Livy's staring.

"That was close," he said. "Mr. Bowen nearly caught me running into the Temple." He frowned as he looked at Livy. "Haven't I seen you somewhere before?"

"No, you haven't"—Celia seemed to be having trouble talking—"she's new."

But Livy recognized the boy. He had handed back her bus pass when she dropped it on the bus, had spoken to the kind book man in the park . . .

Livy copied Celia as she dropped her head and stared at her shoes. But she could feel the boy looking at her from underneath his brown curly bangs.

"I'll remember in a minute," he whispered. "Because I *know* I've seen you before."

Dr. Smythe had started speaking, but Livy, in her embarrassment, took a few seconds to realize that she had no idea what the woman was saying.

"Templar Latin," Celia whispered. "It's different from ordinary Latin so anything you learned at your last school won't be much help." Livy didn't say that no one learned Latin at her last school.

Relieved that she didn't have to listen, Livy kept her head lowered whilst glancing up at the boy called Joe Molyns.

He was staring up at the large stained-glass window set into the side of the Temple. Livy, too, looked up and found herself staring into the pools of colored light. The luminous image was, she thought, beautiful but troubling. There was a tower that looked very like the white tower in the corner of the Court of Sentinels, except that in this painted version, red and white roses wound up and around the pale stones to the gray roof. Around the image were symbols—inverted triangles, crescent moons, circles with arrows through them, more roses that looked as if they had been painted in thick, dark blood . . . And at the top of the tower, instead of a carved stone Sentinel with a broken wing, there was a boy with dark hair stepping across from the tower onto a cloud.

He was looking straight ahead—his hand was outstretched and his fingers almost touched a painted sun and moon as if he was unaware of where he was. Livy squinted to read the letters beneath the boy's foot: *Tempus Fugit*—the same words that she had read on Master Burgess's portrait. But it was the boy's smile that frightened Livy so much her pulse quickened. How could he look so calm? Did he not realize how close he was to the edge of the tower? Did he really think the cloud just beneath his outstretched naked foot would bear his weight?

A black shadow darted behind the boy in the window, then another, and in the next second, the glass exploded as a bird tumbled through the glass.

For a second, it was as if the window tried to hold itself together. The boy was still there on top of the tower, about to step into the sky, except it was now the real sky that Livy could see through the hole in the glass. But then the boy, too, splintered and fell, the breaking glass sounding like an audience laughing. Livy saw the bird's wing catch on the jagged glass and a feather floated lightly down after the heavy pieces.

Someone screamed.

Dr. Smythe dropped her book of Templar Latin to the floor with a great *thud*, her hand flying to her mouth. She seemed too shocked to be able to do anything.

Mr. Bowen leapt up. "Stay calm, everyone!" he shouted. "There is nothing to see!"

But clearly no one agreed with him as they craned their necks and leaned forward to get a better view of the bird desperately trying to fly but managing no more than a sickening falling and swooping movement accompanied by the frantic flapping of wings. It hurled itself at the bottom part of the window, which was still in one piece, then fell, heavy as a stone, to the ground.

"It's dead!" someone shouted.

"Thank you, Nicholas," Mr. Bowen called out. "Helpful as ever."

A few braver pupils laughed. Mr. Bowen frowned and clapped his hands to restore order.

"Quiet, please. We will exit the Temple calmly, starting with the rows nearest the door. Keep moving and keep your eyes straight ahead! There is nothing to see!"

"Except an enormous window in pieces on the floor," Joe whispered.

Livy concentrated on the shattered glass. Sky filled the empty window now, all clouds and lead gray. There was a streak of red—pigeon's blood—on the jagged glass of the window.

That was what she could see now. But she had seen more, hadn't she? There had been two shadows behind the glass, as if something bigger had been chasing the bird into the window . . .

As Livy turned to go, the other pupils still murmuring and straining to look at where the poor bird had fallen, she looked up again at the teachers. Dr. Smythe was staring fixedly at the broken window and the cloud-strewn sky behind. Her face was white with shock. Or anger.

"Quite a dramatic first morning for you, Livy," Amy said as they left the Temple.

"Let's hope it's not an omen," Martha added sweetly.

CHAPTER EIGHT

"Wow!"

"Awesome!"

"Did you see it when it smashed into that pillar?"

"Boof! I thought it would explode!"

"It looked frightened!"

"Nah, stunned."

They were outside, and the voices swirled around.

Livy saw Joe Molyns—now standing a few feet away from her—laughing with a group of his friends.

"I was *so* late," he was saying. "Bowen nearly got me!"

"There he is!" Amy had grabbed Celia's arm and was pulling excitedly on her blazer. "Oh, Celia. You are just made for each other!"

"I've got more pictures." Martha had her phone discreetly angled toward the boy.

Celia was looking at him from underneath her lashes. But the boy, oblivious, took no notice.

"Why didn't you say anything to him, Celia?" Amy asked.

Livy saw that although the question seemed innocent, Amy had exchanged a look with Martha.

"Struck dumb," Celia mumbled. Then she sighed. "He's just too beautiful!"

Dr. Smythe now swept past, a group of stern-faced teachers following her.

"Over four hundred years old," Livy heard one of them say.

"Priceless," added another.

"Given to the school by Master Burgess himself!"

"You can't restore something like that."

Livy and the others picked up their bags from the locker room by Mr. Bowen's office and crossed the Court of Sentinels to the science labs.

Livy wanted to talk about what she had seen before the bird flew into the window, but Amy and Martha were talking to Celia and handing their phones around. More pictures of Joe Molyns, no doubt.

Pupils swarmed in and out of doorways, but there was one doorway that no one entered—the one studded with nails and set into the flint and white stone tower on which the Sentinel with the broken wing stood guard.

The Sentinel that she had stared and stared at ever since they had moved into the house on Leaden Lane and yet had never again seen the feathers move as they had on the day of her interview.

As they drew level with the door, Livy shivered. There were words carved into the stone lintel.

"What does *tempus fugit* mean?" she asked.

She thought of the dark portrait of Master Burgess when Dr. Smythe had told her about his mad ideas about that strange "mortal force," the heaviness in the blood that had brought gravity into the world. And the boy in the stained-glass window, now destroyed, who had stuck out his foot as if he could walk over the words. And now above the door to this tower. What connected them?

"Didn't you learn Latin at your last school?" Martha said.

Celia frowned at Martha and Martha pulled an "I'm sorry" face.

"It means 'time flies,'" Celia explained. "Although whoever it was who carved it on the White Tower had never sat through double math at Temple College!"

"But you're *so* good at math, Celia," Amy said. "You had the highest score on the last test."

"Tied for the best," Celia corrected her. "With Alex."

"Alex is *sooooo* boring." Amy frowned. "He's always staring at me." She sniffed. "As if!"

They pushed past pupils coming down a broad oak staircase in some part of the school that Livy had already forgotten how they had gotten to. Painted faces looked down on her from portraits in heavy gilt frames and every one of those faces seemed to sneer at her. Perhaps those long-dead scholars were right, Livy felt, dropping her eyes. What right had she to be here? Everyone who walked past her seemed so assured, so confident. Livy felt lost and out of place.

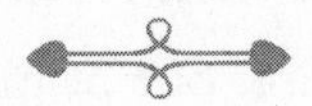

As they found their seats in the classroom, Amy said to Celia, "Pleeeeease sit next to me. You know I'm going to need your help."

"But what about Livy?" Celia said.

"She can sit next to Martha," Amy said, pulling Celia into the seat next to her.

"Do you mind?" Celia looked concerned.

Livy shook her head and moved into the seat behind Celia and Amy.

Martha didn't immediately sit down. Livy could see her scanning the classroom. "Actually, I'd better sit next to Francesca," she muttered and slipped into another seat, leaving Livy on her own.

Livy felt her cheeks turn red. She took out her bashed pencil case and laid it on the desk in front of her.

"Can I sit here?" The thin, pale boy with ragged blond hair who Amy had been so rude to in the Temple stood next to the empty seat.

"Sure," Livy said.

"Who are you?" The boy stuck his bag under the desk. Livy couldn't place his accent.

Amy turned around. "She's called Livy Burgess."

"Burgess?" The boy looked surprised.

"She's new, Alex. Don't get any ideas."

Livy saw the boy's cheeks redden and she felt sorry for him. He got his textbook out of his bag.

"He's from Moscow." Amy smirked. "He came in *first* on the entrance exam." She turned back to Celia and whispered, "Not that it makes up for anything else!"

Celia elbowed Amy in the ribs.

The boy ignored Livy, working furiously on the equations that the teacher wrote on the board. Livy copied them into the book she had been given, but had no clue how to attempt them.

Alex's pen suddenly hovered over her page. "You have to work out what is inside the brackets first," he mumbled.

When the bell rang to signal the end of the lesson, the boy hurriedly put all his things into his bag, then hesitated. "Are you a *real* Burgess?" he asked.

Livy shrugged. "I might be."

The boy looked troubled and left the room quickly.

"Did I say something to upset him?" Livy said.

"Don't take it personally. He's quite a loner," Celia explained.

Amy put her large, expensive, and very definitely designer bag on her shoulder. "Quite a *loser*," she said.

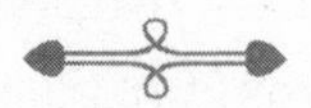

The day's lessons went past in a blur of endless corridors and classrooms; Livy had no idea where she was and made sure that she stuck close to Celia at each lesson change.

Still, she had done it, she thought as the final bell rang out. She had survived a whole day. And nothing too awful had happened. She would have to watch out for Martha and Amy, but Celia looked as if she could handle them. Or ignore them. Which was the same thing.

On the way back to the locker room, Mr. Bowen asked Livy to step into his office.

"Did you find your way around?" he asked kindly. "It's quite easy to get lost in Temple College."

Livy nodded.

"Has Celia been looking after you?"

"Yes, sir," replied Livy, addressing him in the Temple College manner.

"Temple College is a little different from most schools—we have our own way of doing things. But I am sure you will fit in quite nicely." He smiled at her. "Celia will take care of you. Just don't take too much nonsense from the other two."

As Livy entered the locker room, she could hear Amy talking. "Do we *have* to ask her, Celia?"

"But she's new, Amy. Imagine what you would feel like if you started at a strange school and didn't know anyone. I think it would be kind if we invited her. And she seems very nice."

"But we've been dragging her around *all day,*" Martha added. "*Please* don't let's take her for frozen yogurt! She's going to make us look seriously uncool. Have you seen her phone? It's out of the Dark Ages!"

"Shhh!" Amy had looked up to see Livy.

Celia blushed at the awkwardness, but smiled broadly at her. "We're going for frozen yogurt. Do you want to come?"

Livy looked at Martha and Amy, who were standing behind Celia. They weren't smiling.

"I . . . I'll go home, if you don't mind," Livy said.

Martha nodded her approval. Amy's mouth squeezed into a tight smile of triumph.

"Are you sure?" Celia said.

"See you tomorrow," Martha said loudly, turning her back on Livy to put a book in her locker.

"Yeah." Livy shrugged her backpack onto her shoulder.

As she left the locker room, she heard Martha say, "I thought she would never leave!"

And then worse, Celia's reply: "I feel sorry for her. She seems a bit lost."

CHAPTER NINE

Livy put her key in the door.

"There's a snack on the kitchen table . . ." Her mother's voice floated down from upstairs. "Can you pick up Tom from preschool for me in ten minutes? I'm hanging curtains! I'll call them to say that you are coming . . ."

The snack was a large sugary doughnut that made her teeth itch just looking at it. She couldn't face eating anything after her day at school.

"How was it?" her mother called down again. "Did you make friends?"

As if she could make friends in a day! It had taken her almost her entire life to be friends with Mahalia.

"I don't know how many times I have to say this," Livy muttered to herself, cringing at the memory of Celia, Martha, and Amy talking about her in the locker room, "I don't need friends."

Livy shut the front door behind her and ran toward the end of the street. Tom's new preschool was not far; she had to go to the church on the other side of the roundabout and knock on the green door.

"A bit lost." That's what they thought of her. And she was going to have to go into school and do it all again tomorrow! But it was true. She was lost. Or rather, she was . . . between places. She couldn't go back to her old school and yet this new one did not seem to have space for her. Or the right kind of space anyway.

Livy found the preschool—the door had been covered with children's paintings, handprints, and cut-out paper shapes. A large piece of paper had been fixed to the middle of the riot of color and shapes: WE PLAY HERE. Underneath were several attempts at handwriting. Some were just strange circles or crosses with dots and squiggles. Tom had written his very neatly, although it was upside down.

"I got a ballooooon!" Tom yelled as he ran at Livy's knees.

The preschool assistant smiled at him and ruffled his hair. "You're Tom's sister?" she asked. "That's nice. He's a lovely boy." She knelt down so that she was at the same height as Tom. "So here's your balloon for being

such a very good boy on your first day. Remember what I said about holding the string very tight?"

He nodded seriously, his eyes wide.

"Do you want me to hold it for you?" Livy asked. "Until we get home?"

"No. No. No." Tom looked up at her. "It is my balloon and I will hold it." After a glance from the preschool assistant, he added, "Thank you."

Outside the church, Tom walked slowly, holding the string of the balloon away from his body.

"Hold it carefully," Livy said.

"You're not the boss of me!"

It was no use, he wouldn't be told. She would just have to watch him if he was going to get his beloved balloon back safe. But Livy was watching him so carefully that she almost tripped off the pavement.

"Good day!"

She looked up to see a small man wearing a limp brown coat over a brown pinstripe suit. On his head he had a rather battered tweed hat and he was carrying a tatty shopping bag full of books. She was struck by how neatly he was dressed even though the clothes themselves were rather shabby.

"It's you!" Livy gasped. "From the park!" She felt suddenly so pleased to see him—a friendly face after all the difficulty of the day.

The man nodded and smiled. "Alan Hopkins. At your service." His face was thin and gray, quite different from how he had appeared in the park, and he seemed to be struggling with a cough. But his eyes still twinkled.

Tom said loudly, "Mommy says I must not talk to strangers!"

The man looked crestfallen. "Oh, I know," he said. "You're absolutely right. But we're not quite strangers. I've told you my name—"

"Who is the man?" Tom interrupted. "Why is he talking? I do not know him."

Livy and Mr. Hopkins laughed, and then the man put his head to one side. He seemed worried suddenly. "And here you are. Dressed as a Temple College scholar!"

"She's Livy Burgess," said Tom. "Not a scholar. And I am Thomas Burgess."

"Ah, I see," said the man solemnly. "And have you read the book I gave you, Miss Burgess?"

Livy winced. "Not yet," she said.

Not only had she not read it, she didn't know where it was. There were plenty of boxes that still needed to be unpacked since the move. Tom pulled on her hand, anxious to go.

"Well, when you do, consider it a message from a distant friend."

Livy nodded. She had once again the reassuring impression that he knew all about her day—about her feeling so lost and out of place.

"We all need a friend, Miss Burgess," the man said to her, raising his hat. "Good-bye."

Livy clutched Tom's hand as they walked away. *I don't need friends,* she thought again.

Tom started making punching movements with the balloon and laughing as it danced about.

"I could wrap the string around your wrist," she said.

"It is *my* balloon," Tom said. "Not yours. I will hold it tight. Like this . . . Oh!" He had opened his paint-smeared hand in order to close it tighter around the string and in that sliver of a second the balloon had sailed up over his head. He turned his face to the sky. "My balloon!" he cried. "Don't go!"

He twisted his hand out of Livy's and ran after the balloon, jumping, but it was already way above his head.

"Oh, Tom!" Livy ran after him.

"Why has it gone?" he wailed. Livy picked him up and he buried his curly head in her shoulder. "It is *my* balloon and it has flown away. Why can't I reach it?" he whispered, on the verge of tears. "When I want it so *much*?"

CHAPTER TEN

Livy climbed slowly up the stairs to her room, her feet heavy as she thought of how much homework she would have to attempt. Unlike her old school, the teachers at Temple College didn't seem to be making any exceptions for her. She would not be allowed to settle in and find her feet. In fact she was already expected to work at the same furious pace as everyone else. She felt suddenly very tired as a wave of loneliness engulfed her. Who could she talk to?

She pulled out her phone—the phone that Martha had said was from the Dark Ages. But she didn't want to change it; it had pictures of her and Mahalia and she still hadn't deleted Mahalia's contact details. She scrolled over her friend's name. What would she tell her about the day? She pressed the green button and heard the number dial. She knew Mahalia's message by heart but still had a weird little shiver as she heard her friend's voice:

"Hi, it's Mahalia! Just leave me a message and I'll get back to you!" There was a gap here and Mahalia giggled before adding, "Ciao!"

Livy threw herself on her bed. She lay quite still for a moment, staring at the ceiling before turning onto her side.

On the floor next to her bed, her mother had put a box of her books that must have been put in the wrong room in the chaos of their move. Livy could see the book that the man who had introduced himself as Mr. Hopkins had given her.

Consider it a message from a distant friend.

It was such an odd thing to say, and yet she felt that the man understood she needed such a message desperately.

She pulled the book out of the box and traced the shape of the seagull with her finger. Was this book really meant to make her feel better?

She read the first page and sighed. No—just some weird story about a seagull. The book was old and useless, nothing special. It couldn't possibly help her deal with the way her life had been altered.

She caught a movement out of the corner of her eye. Something drifted past the window, too slow for a bird. She glanced up and just caught a blob of red against the darkening sky as it went out of view.

Tom's balloon!

Livy pushed the book to one side, jumped off the bed, and threw open the window. The chill of the evening air caught at her throat and made her feel light-headed. She pushed her face into the dark air but couldn't see the balloon. She dragged her chair to the window, her pulse racing, climbed up, and leaned right out.

Floodlights and Sentinels, clouds banked up high and expectant like an audience. But what were they waiting for? As she pulled her legs onto the ledge and twisted her torso to find a handhold on the window frame, she had an extraordinary feeling of weightlessness, as if, were she to carry on pulling herself through the window, she could get onto the sloping roof at the side.

Yes. She could swing her legs around, use the side of the window to steady herself, and then climb quickly up to the roof. And now. Look! Here she was, clinging to the chimney pots! Looking out across the Court of Sentinels. She could see the shattered window of the Temple.

"Whoooo!" she cried out to the sky. She let go of the chimney pots and raised her arms like wings. "I'm a Sentinel!"

She laughed. It was such a strange feeling, this bubbling up of air in her chest. She hadn't felt like this for so long, not since she could laugh with Mahalia about how she would tell that boy with the black spiky hair that he was "the one."

But she never did get to tell him.

Livy saw the balloon. It was bobbing along the roof of Temple College toward the Sentinel who guarded the tower. The White Tower.

A gust of wind whipped her hair across her face. A second later, the wind had moved along the spine of the roof and caught the balloon. It floated up and hovered a few feet above the tiles.

Livy had two options: She could climb back down into her room or she could walk along the roofs of these narrow little houses until they joined the outer wall of Temple College. She scanned the roofscape. Would it be that hard?

She could hear sirens screaming and the slow growl of London traffic. The air was cold now, and she blew on her fingertips. They were tingling just as they had when she had first arrived at Temple College for her interview.

She watched the balloon. If she was going to go, it would have to be now because in a few more seconds it would float off across the Court of Sentinels toward the Temple.

She ran and, as she ran, she no longer had to watch her step or feel for the tiles under her feet. All she had to do was cut through the air as if she were the blade of a sword or the edge of a bird's wing.

The balloon was up ahead, held still in the folds of stone-carved wings.

Without realizing, she had run toward the Sentinel and now she, too, was on the roof of the White Tower. It was flat here, the roof beneath her feet was covered with lead; she could feel the spine where the metal folded over itself beneath her feet. The circle of dull metal was surrounded by a shallow gully and a wall of three bricks in height. She looked back toward her open bedroom window and her head began to spin. How had she got here so easily?

She reached out toward the stone figure to steady herself and touched the edge of the broken wing.

"Who did this to you?" Livy asked the carved face with the blank expression. "Does it mean that you can't fly?"

This close, the Sentinel was much taller than it had appeared from the ground, even from Dr. Smythe's study. She thought that she could easily sit beneath what remained of his broken wing. She grabbed at one of the spines of the feathers and swung herself around so that she could look up at his face.

"Sorry," she whispered. "I didn't mean to be rough."

She wasn't sure why she spoke, but it seemed that she shouldn't treat him just like a tile on a roof, scrambling over him without a care. Of course he was stone, she told herself, but there was something about that face that seemed so lifelike that she didn't want to think he was no more than a flagstone.

"You should be alive," she whispered, and without thinking she stood on tiptoe and reached up to stroke the Sentinel's beautiful stone cheek. She thought she saw the Sentinel shiver at her touch.

Despite the chill in the dark night air, the stone was warm, like skin.

The heat of the Sentinel made her realize that she was cold. She tucked herself under its wing and stared across the river, made herself see what he saw. How would it feel to have her face always turned in the direction of the setting sun? If she were carved from stone, would she feel the heat of the sun in summer? Would frost make her carved lips crack in winter? She shivered. It was getting colder. She leaned back against the Sentinel's stone gown and immediately felt the chill leave her shoulders.

Soft blurry light from the embankment turned the trees into glowing lollipops. Livy rested her head against the carved folds of the Sentinel's robes. It seemed as if she was being told things of such importance that she had to listen very carefully.

It is time . . . That was what he said, she was sure. And she felt as though those words had been floating here for hundreds of years.

"Of course," she whispered.

She felt herself stand up once more.

She stepped forward and climbed up onto the parapet that ran around the roof of the tower.

The bricks were hardly wide enough for her feet; as she wiggled her toes forward she remembered the summer her father had taught her to dive. They had sat together on the side of the pool. Her father had told her to put her arms above her head and then bend over so that her arms and head were between her knees. And then he had gently tapped her on the back, and she had rolled forward into the cool water. She could still remember the shiver of delight as she realized the very instant that it was *too late* and she couldn't step back from the edge.

It was so simple. She felt the building beneath her feet, immense and solid, but, as she sensed in that moment, no more solid than the air.

Yes.

That was what the Sentinel—because it was the Sentinel, she was sure—was telling her. She looked up at the impassive face, high forehead, and full expressive lips. Those large stone eyes under half-closed lids stared ahead and lichen bloomed on the high cheekbones. There were no words from those lips, of course, the mouth was still. But what she heard, deep in the recesses of her mind, was a language, nonetheless. It was the sound of wings beating, the rush of air through the lungs.

Livy gulped the night deep into her chest and felt how the air was not held in her lungs, but was absorbed into every part of her body. She felt herself dissolve the weight of her body and mix herself with the air.

Should she?

Putting one foot back up onto the ledge, then the other, Livy steadied herself as she stood up. She put one foot forward now, into the air, as if a bridge had appeared before her. Livy smiled and thought about the boy in the window and how she had been worried when he had looked so serene. How stupid she had been! Of course the boy would be happy standing on top of the tower; he had only to step forward and the air would support him. She, too, would step into the air, would feel it become solid under her feet.

Livy looked back at the Sentinel. He looked so noble, so brave, so sure. He seemed entirely alive and weightless even though he was cut from stone.

The air swept up from the ground below. She felt it climb up her body, move over her and through her. It became solid and she knew she could lean against it, tipping even farther forward. It was as if her body was dissolving into the air. The feeling of being both lighter than the air, but somehow the very air itself made the blood jump in her veins.

"I don't need wings," she laughed, "or clouds to step on."

Livy put her arms out in front of her.

She closed her eyes—one breath more—and stepped forward.

CHAPTER ELEVEN

She cried out as she felt a sharp tug on her arm.

What was she doing?

She looked down. Mistake. Her right foot hung in the air high above the flagstones. She had stepped forward, transferred all her weight, and felt the air support her. Hadn't she? And yet here she was, in the split second after it was too late to step back!

And now, as she hung in the air, like a puppet held by a single string, she could feel the air collapse beneath her.

She could hear herself breathing, a ragged sound as if she couldn't get the air into her lungs fast enough. And the air tasted like burning metal. It made her eyes water.

And then she felt herself pulled backward with such force that she fell off the parapet onto the gray lead of the roof.

The cool disc of the moon regarded her with a haughty disdain.

What had she just done?

A sly wind had picked up and she felt suddenly cold, unable to stop her teeth chattering. She crawled across the roof and pressed herself to the Sentinel's stone gown, but it did not warm her. She felt unbalanced, as if she was again in that moment where she had tipped too far forward and would surely fall.

"What was I thinking?" she said, blowing into her hands to try and warm them. She stood up and stamped her feet. She should go. She should never have come. Livy edged her way around the back of the Sentinel, climbed onto the parapet and dropped down onto the outer wall of Temple College. This part was easy because the wall was wide. But when she got to where she must drop down onto the narrow roofs of the houses in the street behind, even though her open window was in sight, she froze. How had she gotten up here? And how would she get back down? Livy hung her feet over the edge and gingerly felt for the tiles below. Once she was on the spine of the roof, she took her time, inching forward over the curved tiles, walking with her arms out like a tightrope walker. She clung to every chimney pot, hardly daring to let go to continue her journey.

But getting down to the window was the worst part. She had to be able to slide down the tiles and then hang on to the window to stop herself falling to the street below. She sat clinging onto the chimney pot and thought about whether it would be better to wait in the cold until morning came and then shout down to someone in the street to help her. But she looked up and kept her eyes on the moon, letting her feet find the way as she slid down to her window.

She almost slipped, caught herself just in time.

Hours later Livy woke with a start, flinging out her arms as if she were falling. Gray morning light filled her tiny bedroom. She wasn't falling, she was lying in her bed.

"Liveee! Liveeeee! You must wake up. You must look with your eyes!"

"No, Tom." Livy groaned, pressing her heavy head deeper into the pillow. "Leave me alone. I'm sleeping."

"But you must see!"

Livy felt a weight moving over her legs and stomach, and felt Tom's hot little hands on her face as he tried to pry open her eyelids.

"Go away, you annoying boy!" she cried. "I don't want to see anything! I want to sleep!"

He sat back on her chest, which made it even harder to breathe.

She opened one eye. "What?"

"My balloon!" Tom looked overjoyed. In his hand was the string of his balloon. He tugged it and the balloon danced.

"Where did you get that?" She tried to sound puzzled when clearly her mother had just got him another balloon while he was asleep.

"It was outside."

She frowned when she saw that someone had tied a small stone to the bottom of the string. And around the stone, loops of red thread.

"Was the balloon on your windowsill?" She forced herself to talk to Tom.

He nodded slowly.

"When you woke up?"

Tom's eyes were like big round buttons, his face serious.

"But who could have done that?"

"Mommy says that she doesn't know. So it's probably Count Zacha. He does lots of secret and powerful things," Tom said wisely. "He is my friend and he said he would find my balloon."

"That's very kind of him," Livy murmured.

Her father roared up the stairs, "Livy! Get up!"

Tom tugged on his balloon once more. "You must get up. I heard Daddy say it to Mommy, too."

"Well, move then, you little idiot!" Livy pushed his body away.

Tom slid off the bed, carefully pulling his balloon along in the air behind him.

"Livy!" Her mother's voice now. "Are you up?"

Her head heavy, she heaved herself into a sitting position. As she did, the book with the seagull on the cover fell to the floor. She picked it up and put it on her bedside table. She would have liked to stay in bed and read whatever was written inside, however useless it might be. Even reading *The Adventures of Count Zacha* would be better than having to go to Temple College to feel stupid and lost.

"Livy!"

Livy grabbed her uniform and tried to shut out the sensation of being on the roof. But as she pulled on her pants, she saw that the skin was rubbed raw on her knees and she felt again how she had climbed up onto the roof tiles and how she had run toward the balloon, feeling lighter with each step.

She tugged yesterday's socks over her heels, did up just two buttons on her blouse, and thrust her feet into her shoes. She felt heavy and out of place once more. There was nothing but a whole day of school ahead of her. How different she felt from those other more confident and accomplished pupils—scholars! She saw Celia being given a lift in some fancy car; she thought of Amy sipping on a fresh smoothie handed to her by a maid; and Martha arranging her hair in a grand gilt mirror, a butler holding a silver tray with hairbrushes and combs laid out for her. And then she imagined Joe Molyns jumping down the steps of his large house and running toward the bus stop. They were all confident, fully themselves. Whereas Livy felt lost and as if she didn't know who she was anymore. She pulled her backpack—*so rustic!*—from the back of her chair and went reluctantly down the stairs. The boy called Alex, though, who had helped her with her math. She couldn't imagine him leaving a large house. Perhaps that was the real reason that Amy and Martha were so mean to him.

"*Tempus fugit*," she said to herself, thinking of the long and lonely day to come. "If only it would."

CHAPTER TWELVE

Livy closed the front door but didn't immediately walk around the corner to Temple College. From the front steps, she looked up at the roofs of the houses in the narrow side street. She scanned the route she thought she must have taken the night before, following the clusters of chimney pots until she reached the wings of the stone creature, his face turned to look over the Court of Sentinels. It was impossible that she had managed without falling to her death. It was too high and too narrow for anyone to have got across. But even as she decided it was impossible, she felt again how easy it had been. She had not given any thought to what she was doing until she had tried to get back to her bedroom.

And who had pulled her back? Because someone had. She could still feel that sharp tug on her arm.

How could she make sense of what had happened?

She couldn't. She hadn't really thought about it at all. It was her body that seemed so sure; every part of her had wanted to step into the sky, and she would have . . . if she had not been pulled back.

She needed to talk to someone, to explain how she had felt. But who? Who would even believe that she had climbed out the window and run along the roof?

Perhaps it would be better just to find someone who could tell her that she was wrong.

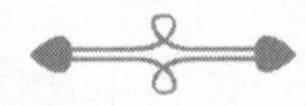

Celia, Martha, and Amy were waiting for Livy on the steps to Burgess. Celia smiled and waved to her.

"I tried texting you last night," she said. "But you didn't reply. Did you manage all your homework?"

Livy, seeing Amy and Martha looking at her closely, nodded, although she had not been able to concentrate on her French composition after climbing back in from the roof. She had scarcely managed to crawl onto her bed and lie there as the room spun around her.

"Miss Burgess?" The school secretary, Miss Lockwood, bustled up to them. "You're needed in Dr. Smythe's study now."

"It's only your second day!" Amy said, her eyes round with surprise. "What *could* you have done?"

As Livy turned away she heard Martha whisper, "She's murdered fashion!"

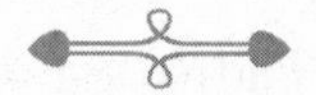

Livy dragged her feet; they felt as heavy as the blood weighing down her veins. What could she have done to cause her to be summoned like this? She looked again at the certificates that lined the stairs. They looked impressive with their gold lettering and gold medallions stamped onto the thick paper.

The door was ajar and Livy could see Dr. Smythe standing to the side of her desk. She was looking at the portrait of Master Burgess.

"Come in!" Dr. Smythe's voice rang out even before Livy's knuckles had touched the wood.

Dr. Smythe turned and seated herself behind her enormous desk. The Sentinel filled the window. The Sentinel that Livy had stood next to last night, whose wing had shivered when she had touched it.

"Don't stand in the doorway," Dr. Smythe called to her.

Livy edged forward, keeping her gaze away from the Sentinel.

Dr. Smythe indicated for Livy to take a seat. Peter Burgess looked down at her, his painted face impassive, unreadable.

"I saw you talking to someone on the street yesterday evening," Dr. Smythe began. "A man wearing a hat and a brown suit?"

Livy started. She hadn't seen Dr. Smythe watching her—was she everywhere? "I don't think we were in any danger," she muttered.

"What did he want? Did he ask you for money?"

Livy shook her head.

"And he didn't threaten you in any way?"

"No. Of course not," Livy said, surprised.

"But he spoke to you."

Livy nodded.

Dr. Smythe made a soft "tut-tutting" noise. "And what did he say?" She picked up a pen and started making notes on a small pad of paper. "Exactly."

"Not much." Livy frowned. She didn't feel like telling Dr. Smythe about the book she had been given, as a gift from a distant friend. It would sound too silly.

Dr. Smythe underlined something twice on her pad. Her handwriting was all curls and flowing lines, and Livy, normally quite adept at reading things upside down, couldn't understand it.

"Did the man speak to Tom at all?" Dr. Smythe said.

"No. He just told us his name."

"I think we don't need to involve the police at this

point," Dr. Smythe said. "But perhaps if the man approaches you again, you will tell me first?" She frowned. "Can you do that?"

Livy nodded.

"And don't speak to him," Dr. Smythe added. "Don't tell him anything. And if he asks for anything . . ."

"Like money?" Livy offered.

"Like money," Dr. Smythe nodded. "Or anything that he could sell . . ."

"I don't think he's capable of doing anything bad at all," Livy blurted out.

Dr. Smythe made a cage out of her fingers and placed her chin on it. There was a streak of black dust on the inside of her wrist, just where the cuff of her white blouse stopped. She must have seen Livy noticing it because she discreetly tugged on her sleeve and the mark was covered.

"The man I saw you talking with is the ex-librarian of Temple College."

"Mr. Hopkins was the librarian?" Livy thought about the man's well-cut suit and his neat appearance, shabby as the clothes were. So this was the man that Celia had said Dr. Smythe had fired. He had been thrown out of his house, too. The house that her family was now living in. How awful! How could Dr. Smythe have been so heartless?

"You feel sorry for him?" Dr. Smythe pursed her lips. "Well, don't. The man is a menace."

"He's not!" Livy said, feeling her voice rise. "He's nice!"

"I think I should be the judge of that." Dr. Smythe looked down at her notes and her golden hair fell across her face. "Thank you, Livy, you can go. You've been most helpful."

CHAPTER THIRTEEN

Livy walked slowly down the stairs past Dr. Smythe's many certificates. Why was she so interested in what poor Alan Hopkins had said to her? And why would she think that the man was a menace?

"Livy!" Celia was standing at the bottom of the stairs. "What are you doing here?"

"I told Mr. Green that I didn't feel well. I had to come and find you. I couldn't bear the suspense! And this has nothing to do with the fact that Mr. Green is the most boring teacher ever!" She squeezed Livy's arm. "Tell me! What did Dr. Smythe want?" Celia looked serious. "You're not in any trouble, are you?"

Livy shook her head. "Dr. Smythe saw the old librarian talking to me yesterday, after school. She wanted to know what he said."

Celia frowned. "Why would Dr. Smythe care?" she said. "She got rid of him, after all."

"Yes," said Livy slowly. "She did."

The bell rang for the change of lesson as they stepped out into the Court of Sentinels.

Celia stood quite still. Joe Molyns was just a few feet away. "I knew I'd see him," she whispered. "I could feel it in my blood."

"Have you ever said anything to him? About how you feel?" Livy said. That was something Mahalia had wanted to do and never got the chance.

"Um, no!" Celia said, looking astounded. "Why would I go and do something like that?"

"Because he might like you, too."

"But he doesn't have a clue who I am! Imagine it, Livy. I pluck up the courage to say something—"

"What would you say?" Livy interrupted her.

"Something like"—Celia's cheeks were scarlet, as if she were actually speaking to Joe—"Hi . . . I saw you play soccer . . . No . . . Hi . . . I'm Celia and . . ." She shook her head. "He's not going to be very impressed!"

"How about if you spoke to him at the bus stop? Just ask him the time. Anything."

"But . . ."

"Just say it to him. What are you worried about?"

"That he would just laugh in my face and walk off. Or worse, much worse, that he would ignore me."

"You could get on the same bus and sit near him?" Livy thought of the jostle to find a seat near Mahalia's crush.

"Martha and Amy would be watching," Celia whispered. "And anyway, they're so much prettier than me. He's bound to want to talk to them!"

"He wouldn't," Livy said.

"Like you're the expert." Celia laughed.

Although Celia asked Livy again if she wanted to join them for frozen yogurt after school, Livy saw how relieved Martha and Amy were when she declined.

"I'm going to see my dad in the library," she improvised.

As Livy walked through the college garden toward the library, she thought about why Celia hung around with Martha and Amy. Livy had known plenty of girls like them in her last school, but she and Mahalia had been such good friends they could ignore the shiny girls. But perhaps Celia didn't notice; they were always really nice to her. And they had so much in common: adoring Joe Molyns.

She found her father's office, not much more than a cubicle, just inside the front door.

"How's the job going?" Livy said to her father's back.

"Second day in and it's already impossible." Her father glanced back and smiled at her, although he looked tired.

"This place is a mess," he went on. "I just went to find a book on gravity that Dr. Smythe has requested—a rare book by our supposed ancestor, Peter Burgess—but someone's been playing tricks and replaced it with a 1970s RV catalog." Livy's father waved a battered magazine in front of Livy and then threw it on the desk in disgust. "RVs! Honestly, Mr. Hopkins has got a lot to answer for. I don't blame Dr. Smythe for getting rid of him. He clearly had no idea what he was doing or how to look after books."

"I could go and look," Livy said. "See what I can find."

"Don't go too far," her father said, speaking to the screen. "It's a labyrinth and you don't have a ball of string. Take a wrong turn in here and you might not come back for a year!"

"Where does that go?" Livy said, pointing to a metal staircase that twisted up to a narrow slanting doorway.

Her father looked up. "Botany," he said, turning back to the computer screen and absentmindedly reaching for a cookie. "I think. Now, where was I?"

Livy climbed the metal staircase, going round and round. At the top, she looked down at her father's head, his hair messy and the collar of his shirt caught in his crumpled sweater.

"Call me when it's time to go," she yelled.

Her father waved his hand in absentminded agreement.

She drifted through a series of small rooms all lined with books. She thought about how Celia had come to find her after she had seen Dr. Smythe, but then left her on her own at lunchtime. True, Celia had apologized later—there had been an art club that she needed to go to and she had been sure that Amy would have looked after her. But Amy hadn't got the text. Apparently. And Martha never ate lunch on a Tuesday. So Livy had sat with her tray in the enormous dining hall, staring at the food she didn't want to eat, avoiding Mr. Bowen's concerned expression as he looked down from the high table where the teachers ate. Livy had wished that she could dissolve. Alex, the quiet Russian boy, had joined her and slowly eaten a slice of pizza, but had not said a word, not even looked in her direction. Livy sighed. She longed to be back in the time and place where friendship was not something she had to watch for every minute of the day.

The floorboards creaked underfoot and the small panes of the mullioned windows made the dusk fall at her feet like a velvet patchwork.

I'll see how far I can get, Livy thought, *before Dad calls me.*

She played the game she and Mahalia used to play. Closing her eyes, Livy ran her finger along a bookshelf. When she opened her eyes, she took whatever book she had found off the shelf and examined it.

"Urgh!" she groaned when she picked out the first one. "It's the periodic table!" She closed it with a snap and shoved it back onto the shelf.

"Not funny, Mahalia," she whispered. "Choose me a nice book."

She closed her eyes, bumped into a bookshelf, corrected herself, and, her finger still trailing along the bookshelves, felt the bookshelf stop and a doorway appear to her touch. She stepped through, almost tripping down a shallow step into the next room, her eyes still closed.

When she next opened her eyes, she was aware of a person in the room. She held her breath and dipped behind a bookcase.

Sitting at a table, surrounded by piles of books, was Alex. His hair stuck up as if he had recently raked it with his fingers. He had loosened his tie and his Adam's apple stuck out as if he had swallowed a walnut. He was writing furiously in a notebook and flicking the pages backward and forward as if he had lost something in the tangle of words.

"Hello." Livy stepped out from behind the bookcase.

Alex jumped. He looked panicked as he pulled the books toward him. "Don't tell your dad I'm here," he whispered.

"Why would I tell my dad? He's a librarian. He likes people to read!"

The boy looked relieved.

"What are you reading?" Livy took a step forward.

Alex looked nervous and put his arm across the old book with thick black type that he had been reading. "I . . . I am doing research," he said.

"What on?"

"History," Alex muttered, moving the books around so that the book he had been reading was now at the bottom of a pile. "It interests me. I want to know what *tempus fugit* means. I have searched through all these books and I can't find the answer."

"Oh, but that's simple," Livy said. "It means 'time flies.' It's Latin."

The boy stared at her with disdain. "I know that!" he muttered. "Do you think I'm stupid? Are you like Martha and Amy?"

"I don't think you're stupid," Livy said quickly.

"The words *tempus fugit* mean something more than just 'time flies,' I am sure." He seemed embarrassed at his outburst and his cheeks had colored. "Because why are they written all over the school? And always they point to Master Burgess . . ." He put his head down and stared at his studies. "Although"—he looked up again, attentive, like a bird—"perhaps you might have some idea. When I asked Mr. Hopkins, he said that only a real Burgess would know. And you're a real Burgess!"

"I have no idea," Livy said.

"It's such a shame that Dr. Smythe got rid of Mr. Hopkins. Now I don't have anyone to ask. Your dad doesn't seem to know anything. Sorry," he added.

"My dad is a really good librarian," Livy said. "I'm sure he'll know more than Mr. Hopkins in no time."

Alex made a face. "Unlikely. Mr. Hopkins had been here for forty years. He knew everything—every book and every scientific paper. Did you know that all the notes of all the scientists who were educated here are kept in this library? It's all part of the Temple College collection!" Alex's cheeks were flushed with excitement. "Apart from Peter Burgess. There's hardly anything of Peter Burgess's work. I asked Mr. Hopkins and he said there was nothing. But isn't that odd? The founder of the school and no one can find out anything about his experiments."

"I suppose . . ." Livy said. "And yet Dr. Smythe seemed to know stuff about him. She told me she had found out about him when she worked in Prague."

Alex looked surprised. "When did she say that?"

"At my interview."

"What did she find out?"

"She said he was rich and paid for some poor boys to be educated here. He paid for the Sentinels and he bought lots of books for the library."

"But nothing about his experiments?" Alex looked hopeful.

"She mentioned the Garden of Eden . . . and angels." Livy shrugged. "I can't really remember. It didn't make much sense to me."

Alex looked down at his books. "Very scientific," he muttered sounding unimpressed. Livy had disappointed him with her meager information.

"Bye, then," Livy said as the silence became longer.

Alex didn't look up. "Bye."

Livy continued with her game, walking farther and farther, bumping into doorways and bookshelves. Why had Dr. Smythe been so intent on getting rid of Mr. Hopkins? And what was it about her father that meant that he had been installed in the job so quickly? Dr. Smythe knew about Peter Burgess's experiments and yet Mr. Hopkins told the woman that there was nothing written by him in the library. Perhaps Mr. Hopkins had been hiding something . . .

These questions went round and round in Livy's mind with no conclusion. She carried on trailing her finger along the shelves, forgetting that she had been walking for some time. When Livy next opened her eyes she felt a tug of panic. Surely she had not walked so far? Looking around, she realized she was quite lost.

The room she found herself in was small and dim, with a half-open door ahead of her. Just as she turned to try and find her way back to her father, she heard footsteps in the room directly above and the sound of something dropped on the floor. A minute later, she thought she heard a voice muttering on the other side of the bookshelf.

She peered around the other side: no one.

The footsteps were behind her now, quick and light. Had she gone too far this time with her games? Livy ducked behind a bookcase as the footsteps came closer, and peered through the gap between the books and the shelf above. She heard a voice, a voice that she recognized, muttering, "Where *is* it?"

And then the quick tapping of high heels, heading back to the stairs.

Livy left the small room and followed the sound of voices to her father's office below. She crept down a few steps and saw two heads, close together. She made herself very still, feeling as if she could almost dissolve into the air. She listened.

"I am concerned that this book is missing, James." Dr. Smythe's voice coiled up toward Livy. "Are you sure you can't find it?"

"I've looked everywhere," Livy's father said, sounding worried. "Could the last librarian have done something with it? The library catalog is in a mess and books have been moved."

"But Alan Hopkins would never have dared to take it," Dr. Smythe said, her voice firm. She brushed her heavy pale hair out of her face, and Livy caught a glimpse of the gold charm bracelet. "I must find out about Peter Burgess's very last experiment! I must find his notes. That book is the only way. It *must* be found, James! That is your job, after all."

Livy heard the woman's heels tapping on the wooden floor. The door of the library closed.

Why was Peter Burgess's notebook so important to Dr. Smythe? And why was she so interested in what Mr. Hopkins knew? What was the woman trying to do?

Slowly, Livy went down.

"Are you really in a lot of trouble if you can't find the book she wants?" she asked.

"I won't be in any trouble." Her father smiled, but he looked sad rather than excited about his dream job. "But I just have to find it," he said, so quietly that Livy could hardly hear him. "I don't have any choice."

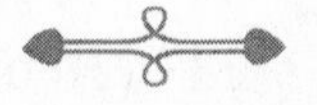

Livy climbed up to her room. The book that the librarian had given her was still on her bedside table. She traced the shape of the seagull once more. She felt so sorry for the man; it was terrible that Dr. Smythe had fired him and thrown him out of his house. That seemed wrong. But perhaps he had been very bad at his job. He was making her father's life difficult, certainly. And how could this

book about a seagull—how could any book—possibly help her?

She looked up. The Sentinel with the broken wing was lit by the soft glow of the streetlights below. He was holding his head as if he were listening to something.

"Hello?" Livy whispered. "Can you hear me?"

Wanting to feel light, weightless, as she had when she ran across the roof, Livy flung open the window, leaned out so that she could see the feathers on the Sentinel's broken wing, and let the air absorb her. The moon was being dragged along by a row of clouds, like horses pulling a silver carriage. She took a deep breath of the night air.

"I know you can hear me," she whispered. And she thought she saw the Sentinel dip his head in agreement and shake his broken wing.

Seconds later, she was scrabbling across the tiles, chasing the last of the day that slipped behind the roof. "I must be careful," she told herself, but she noticed that the less she cared whether she fell, the easier her path, the faster she could slip through the air. The heaviness that had fastened around her after the day at school lifted into the air like smoke. "This is like walking on a tightrope." She lifted her leg in front of her. "I might try a cartwheel, like in the circus!" She lengthened her stride and laughed as she hung in the air between each careless step.

Another leap and she was on the roof of the White

Tower. She drew the night air into her lungs and it made her feel even lighter.

She went right up to the edge of the tower and leaned over. Had she really done this the night before? She remembered that strange sensation of how she felt the air had been solid and she could push herself into it and not fall.

She leaned a little farther, a little farther . . . She felt her heels rise up off the dull lead that covered the roof. Humans could not fly. So why did she feel as if her blood was made of air and that she could step forward and not fall? Even as her head told her she was wrong to feel this way, her heels had lifted and she was climbing up onto the parapet.

Now her toes were right on the edge. She lifted her arms and leaned forward and felt no fear. A breeze swirled around her, and she had the uncomfortable sensation that the Sentinel had just shaken out its wings. That someone was watching her.

"No." She heard a voice right next to her. "I won't let you."

A strange bitter smell, like burning metal, filled her nostrils, and she felt herself thrown back. She landed against the smooth stone of the Sentinel's gown.

"What were you thinking? To stand on the edge like that! Again!"

A boy stood above her.

She was so startled that she couldn't answer.

"Did you think you wouldn't fall?" he said angrily.

"Where did you come from?" Livy gasped. She looked around, confused. The roof was too small for her not to have noticed him. "Have you been watching me?"

The boy did not reply immediately. He stared at her intently, as if he was thinking what he should say. He was taller than her, and very thin. But he could not have been more than two, possibly three years older. He had a narrow face with high, sharp cheekbones and his mouth, although it was full and red, was set in a serious expression. His skin was very pale, like moonlight, and in stark contrast to the inky blackness of his eyebrows and hair. His pale face seemed to float above a loose white shirt and a long black overcoat; one of the buttons had come loose and was hanging by a red thread. The gold flecks in his eyes burned.

"Why are you staring at me like that?" Livy said. "What are you doing here?"

"The same as you." The boy lifted his chin. "I don't belong down there." Livy noticed he spoke with a strange accent that she didn't recognize.

"You remind me of someone." The boy spoke very quietly now.

"Who?"

He shook his head. "Someone from a long time ago. Someone far away."

"Well, I'm just Livy Burgess," Livy said. "No one special."

As she said these words, the boy looked suddenly shocked. "Oh, you should leave Temple College," he said. "Go and not come back!" He stepped back from her. "You're the wrong element. You will spoil everything! You Burgesses made trouble before! Your experiments, your ideas . . ."

A bird swooped into Livy's face and she put her hands up and ducked. She felt the bitter air stir around her and heard the bird fly away, its wings singing.

When she dropped her hands, she was alone. The boy was gone. He must have slipped behind the row of chimney pots.

But how would he get down? Was there some other, easier, way up to the roof?

I don't belong down there.

He'd been angry with her, but he'd also made her feel better. There was someone else who was struggling to feel that they belonged.

And who do I remind him of? Livy felt as if her brain was frowning with the effort of trying to think about the boy's strange words. It was odd, because she, too, felt that she had met the boy before. As if he was a friend that she had, until the very moment when he had spoken to her, forgotten that she had, one who was angry about something she had done. But what?

"Tom!" she cried as she dropped down from the window ledge into her room. "You should be asleep."

Her little brother was sitting on the side of her bed in his pajamas. He made no comment on the fact that she had just climbed in through the window.

"Did you see Count Zacha?" he said. "On the roof?"

"Count Zacha?" Livy turned and closed the window. "Of course not!" But her pulse had jumped. Had Tom been watching her?

She picked him up firmly. "Time for bed."

"I can see him."

"Yes, yes," Livy sang.

"In the sky. He flies past my window."

"Of course he does," Livy agreed—always the best option if you didn't want Tom to make a fuss.

"Your face is as cold as the sky," Tom whispered as he put his arms around her.

"And you are very tired," Livy said. "It's too late for a little boy like you to be awake."

"I am not a little boy." Tom shook his head. "I am a flying fighter like Count Zacha!"

"Even Count Zacha needs to go to bed," Livy said. She carried him down the stairs to his bedroom. The house was silent, her parents already asleep.

"Count Zacha never sleeps." Tom yawned as Livy tucked him in. "He told me."

CHAPTER FOURTEEN

Livy spent the next day in a daze. She heard people talk to her and answered them; she did her work in class without too much staring out the window. She again sat next to Alex when he slipped into the seat next to her while Celia was chatting. He again helped her to find the answers, but without saying anything and with his cheeks permanently flushed. Livy noticed this, but felt disconnected. All the while there was a part of her that was trying to make sense of what had happened on the roof the night before. That part of her mind was filled with the light night air, the bright silver moon, and a boy's gold-flecked green eyes.

Who was he?

And why had he spoken to her in that angry and perplexing way? *Did you think that you wouldn't fall?* Livy shivered as she remembered his voice, full of moonlight. But stern, too, as if he really cared about her. She put her hand up to her cheek as though she could stop herself blushing. She groaned. How could she have been so stupid? *I should have said something,* she thought. *I should have thought of something clever or funny, something impressive that would have made him think that I am brave and clever and different from anyone else he had ever met.* She realized that she should have said something that would have made him want to be her friend. But—of course!—she had been too shocked to say anything other than to ask him where he came from!

Amy clicked her fingers in Livy's face as they went up the oak staircase. "Hello?" she said. "Earth to Livy!"

Martha, her hair today in a glossy sheet held back by a thin hair band, nudged her. "Are you OK, Livy?" She sounded concerned. "Amy! Don't you think Livy looks really, really pale?"

Amy squinted. "White as a sheet."

Celia looked worried. "You do look pale. Did you sleep OK?"

"Yes!" Livy said, trying out a small laugh that was intended to make her appear carefree. "Of course!" she said. "I slept like a log."

But Martha, with her ridiculous fussing, had broken the spell, and Livy would have to recreate the picture that had been so vivid in her mind. She focused on the sharp smell of the night air, the moon hanging low over the river, and the Sentinel's broken wing. She felt her stomach turn as she remembered how she had leaned so far over the parapet and allowed her heels to rise up off the lead. And the boy—he now filled her mind with his moon-white skin, black hair, and piercing green eyes. She avoided Celia's intrusive gaze as his words rang in her ears. *I don't belong down there.* Those words meant that there was someone else who felt as out of place as she did. Someone else who only felt alive when they could reach out and brush the sky with their fingertips.

But what could he have meant by those angry words, *You Burgesses . . .*? What trouble could any Burgess have caused? And, even more stinging: *You're the wrong element.* What did he know about her feeling out of place? She had told no one.

Standing outside a classroom as she waited for the pupils to come out, their voices loud and confident, she felt suddenly very alone even though she was surrounded by a crush of bodies. She could, surely, just allow her body to float up to the roof. Perhaps the boy would be there, waiting for her, and she would be able to convince him that she was no trouble to him. That they were the same. Maybe she would even be brave enough to tell him that she had never before felt such a strange sensation when she had met someone, as if they had already met. She shook her head. Where could she have met him?

And when? She had no clear recollection of it. She thought again about his strange clothes—they looked as if he had found them in a costume box. And his accent—she had lived in London all her life but had never heard words pronounced that way, like small hammers striking metal.

"Does the school have a janitor?" Livy asked Celia.

Celia looked surprised. "There's a maintenance department," she said. "Why?"

"I just wondered if the janitor had a son who lived at the school."

Celia was staring at her closely, her large violet eyes troubled. She shook her head. "I've never seen anyone who looks as if they might be the janitor's son. Why do you ask?"

Livy shrugged her shoulders and tried out her new fake carefree laugh again. "I don't know. I just wondered."

If only I could get up on the roof right now, she thought. *I would make that boy understand how I feel. Because he's right. I really don't fit in down here.*

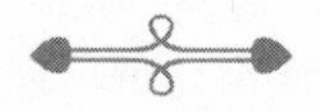

Livy felt no more included by the end of the morning; all the other pupils seemed to accept the formality and the rules, seeming to revel in the sensation that this made Templars somehow superior.

In the line for the dining hall at lunchtime, Celia explained, "We do this Rich Scholar Poor Scholar lunch once a week since Dr. Smythe turned up. If you get a poor lunch, it's meant to make you feel like the poor boys that Peter Burgess educated at his own expense. Those boys must have been half starved! Take a ticket and hand it in. You'll be told which lunch to take."

Livy was distracted by laughter. Joe Molyns could not keep a straight face as his friends took handfuls of tickets in the hope that they might get a decent lunch. Perhaps that was why, having handed in her ticket, Livy took the wrong tray.

"You had a Poor Scholar ticket," Celia whispered, her eyes sliding toward the older boys. "You've got the Rich Scholar lunch. Quick! You have to put it back! Dr. Smythe is staring at you!"

Livy put the tray laden with food back, her cheeks flaming as the group of boys behind them—including Joe Molyns—turned to look. Mahalia would have said that she wanted the ground to swallow her. But Livy hoped for the sky—that she could just dissolve like smoke and drift upward.

"She's new," Celia explained in a tiny voice.

"It happens," Joe said cheerily. "We were all new once."

Celia turned away, overcome. Sheepishly, Livy picked up the right tray on which there was just a piece of dark bread and a bowl of thin, gray-looking soup, no more appetizing than a puddle.

"Hey!" She turned to see Joe Molyns standing behind her, with his Rich Scholar tray. "Why not take mine?" He shoved the tray at her and the soup splashed out.

"No. Thank you. Really. Very kind. Not hungry."

"Of course you are. I've got soccer practice in five minutes. I'll never have time to eat all this."

Livy knew what was happening as he started piling plates onto her tray. The capillaries in her cheeks were expanding and filling with blood. Her face would be scarlet.

"That's it!" Joe exclaimed. "I knew it! The bus! We had a conversation about gravity! I knew I'd seen you somewhere before!"

He picked up Livy's bowl of soup and put it down on his tray, spilling half of the thin, gray liquid. "I never forget a face!" And then, Livy already forgotten, he turned to join his friends at their table.

"You saw Joe on the bus?" Celia whispered as they went to join Martha and Amy. "And had a conversation about gravity?" Her eyes were round. "I've never had an actual conversation with Joe. Apart from just now. But I only said a few words and then my brain exploded and I couldn't think of anything else to say."

"I dropped my bus pass, that's all," Livy said. "It wasn't what I would call a conversation."

"Celia!" Martha said, patting the bench next to her. "Come and tell us all about it."

Celia frowned. "He helped Livy when she got confused about lunch." She stared at Joe's back. "He's so kind."

Livy remembered how Mahalia had said a similar thing about her crush when all the boy had done was offer his friend some chewing gum.

"Oh no," Amy said, dropping her gaze. "Here comes Alex. He's staring straight at me! Don't look up. Don't give him any encouragement."

Under her lashes, Livy saw Alex stop next to her. He didn't seem interested in Amy at all. He stared at the empty place, but when Livy didn't look up, he walked quickly away.

"That's right, move along and sit with the freaks and the geeks," Martha said.

"So *uncool*. Thinking he was welcome here." Amy smirked.

"What's wrong with him?" Livy said, feeling angry with herself for stupidly doing what Amy had told her to.

"What's wrong with him?" Amy said in mock surprise. "What's *right* with him?"

Livy wanted to apologize to Alex for the way he had been treated at lunchtime—for the way she had been so cowardly—and say that she would have liked him to join them, but he just scowled at her as they waited outside the classroom before going in for their science lesson.

They heard Dr. Smythe's heels in the corridor and the pupils, who had been chatting and laughing, unpacking their bags, or lounging across desks, went quiet when the headmistress walked briskly into the classroom. Pupils shifted in their seats and sat up straight as she took her place in front of them. "Good afternoon," she said, and the class mumbled a ragged, "Good afternoon, Dr. Smythe," back at her.

Her golden hair was pulled back into a neat bun, and her gray suit, tailored and tight fitting, made her body look as if she had been dipped in a dull metal. "So chic," Celia whispered.

Dr. Smythe leaned against the teacher's desk at the front of the room and looked around the class. No one moved.

"Last week we talked about some of the scientists who have been educated at Temple College. We spoke about Emily Woodstock. Can anyone remember why she was important?"

Celia put her hand up. "The first woman to be accepted at Temple College. She researched the effects of magnetic fields, building on Michael Faraday's pioneering work."

"Very good, Celia. Now, today I want us to think about the most visionary scientist that Temple College has produced—the founder of Temple College, Peter Burgess. Does anyone know why he was so important?"

No one replied. After a few seconds, Dr. Smythe said, "Livy, do you have any idea?"

Livy heard Alex shift in his seat behind her. "Blood," he whispered.

But Livy felt awkward and shook her head. Dr. Smythe had spoken about Peter Burgess in her interview, something to do with the Garden of Eden, but she couldn't remember exactly what had been said.

"He wrote about something he called a mortal force that pulled all objects toward the surface of the earth. What does that sound like? Alex?"

"Gravity, Dr. Smythe."

"Creep," Livy heard Amy mutter to Martha.

"Peter Burgess also believed that there was a living force inside us that filled our body with air. What does that sound like? Amy, why don't you tell us?" Dr. Smythe stared at Amy, who fiddled with her pen. "Perhaps I will ask Alex again as he has been paying attention. Alex?"

"Blood, Dr. Smythe."

"Excellent. Peter Burgess carried out many experiments on this living force. Do you have any idea how he collected samples of blood?"

"He used leeches," Alex blurted out.

"Indeed. You are very knowledgeable, Alex. Leeches, for those who don't know their medical history, are a sort of worm found in the river. They were placed on the skin and they would suck blood until they became full and fell off."

"Urgh," Celia said beneath her breath.

"A rather ingenious way of collecting fresh blood samples for Peter Burgess's scientific work! He was a daring and visionary early scientist."

Alex coughed.

"Peter Burgess understood that science is about asking questions and then designing experiments to answer those questions. What I want you to do now is to think about a big question or problem you would like to solve, and then devise the most daring experiment you can. And tell me how you would go about it. Be brave! Shoot for the stars! You may not have the ability to talk to angels, as Master Peter Burgess believed he had, but you may come up with something interesting. Try and think about the challenges the world is facing—there are many—and find a solution. Surprise me!"

Livy's hand hovered over the paper of her notebook.

What would she change if she could? Well, that was easy . . .

"I'm going to write about artificial intelligence," she heard Amy say. "It's *got* to be the way we solve things in the future. Wars and stuff."

"What about you, Livy?" Celia asked.

Livy felt awkward. "A cure for leukemia," she muttered.

"Boring," Martha mouthed.

Livy turned away. She wouldn't risk telling them about how she wanted to find a way of taking all the bad things out of a child's tainted blood and altering it until it became strong and healthy.

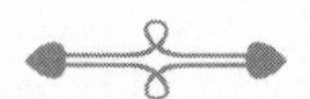

As they left the classroom, Livy found Alex walking at her shoulder. Amy giggled to Martha.

"Why does Dr. Smythe always speak of Peter Burgess as if he was this amazing scientist?" Alex asked Livy. "She says he did all these experiments, but where is the proof? I could say that I discovered uranium, or plutonium, or . . . or . . . *cheese* if I didn't have to prove it!"

Livy looked at his ragged blond hair. The collar on his shirt was too big and his blazer pocket was torn. She was surprised at the intense look on Alex's face. "It's

not just Dr. Smythe, Alex. Everyone thinks Peter Burgess is a legend."

"Livy?" They both turned to see Dr. Smythe standing in the doorway. "Your essay?"

Livy blushed as she pulled her book from her bag and handed it to Dr. Smythe. She felt awkward; no one else had had to hand in work. The woman flipped it open and scanned the opening paragraph. Livy held her breath. This was excruciating.

"Interesting." Dr. Smythe smiled. "You want to find a cure for leukemia? A noble cause, indeed." She closed the book. "I think you should pursue these ideas, Livy, and we can discuss them in our next lesson. In the meantime . . ." She slipped the book into her sleek red leather briefcase. "I'd like to read this in more detail."

"Weird," Alex said as Dr. Smythe disappeared. "She never bothers marking anything. What's got her so interested?" He made a face. "I mean it's not as if you're going to find a cure for *anything!*"

But, Livy thought as they walked slowly down the corridor, *if I could find a cure . . .* She saw herself standing up in class and explaining how she had devised an experiment that could miraculously transform diseased blood, and smiled as she imagined Dr. Smythe's admiring expression.

"Uh-oh." Alex nudged her. Livy looked at him, surprised he was still walking alongside her. "Forget it."

"Forget what?"

"You're twelve, remember? Twelve-year-olds don't find cures for anything!"

Livy left the others in intense discussions over whether they should follow Joe Molyns to the bus stop.

"I've got lip gloss," Amy whispered to Martha as Celia was busy swapping her books in her locker. "Your favorite shade. We'll look super cute for Joe."

"Are you sure you won't come?" Celia said to Livy, oblivious.

"She's really tired, can't you see?" Martha was brushing her long hair and the static made the hairbrush make odd scratching noises. "It's probably very tiring starting a new school." She smiled at Livy, but Livy understood what the girl really meant.

"Does anyone have any lip gloss?" Celia asked. "My lips are so dry."

"Amy's got some," Livy said. Amy glared at her. Livy ignored her. "I'm sure it will make you look super cute."

"Come on, let's go." Amy pushed past Livy. "I'll give it to you on the way."

Livy was relieved. She wanted to be alone with her thoughts about the roof of the White Tower, the Sentinel, and a boy who was not confident, popular Joe Molyns. The girls would laugh at her, she was sure. And even if Celia was kind to her and took her seriously, telling her would make it less real, less hers. She didn't want to share the roof with anyone.

CHAPTER FIFTEEN

That night on the roof the moon hung ahead of her like a silver coin tossed into the sky. The chimney pots cast dark shadows, true "moon shadows." Livy skipped over them as if they were puddles. She stopped halfway to catch her breath. Or perhaps it was her body that she needed to catch, because she felt as light as the air itself. Surely, if she let go of the chimney stack, she could float over the roof toward the Sentinel as easily as Tom's red balloon. She let go of the bricks and chased the clouds, kicking the night air with her heels.

Out of the corner of her eye, she caught a flicker of movement in the street below. She dropped down behind the next chimney stack, her heart pounding in her chest. Had she been seen? She peered around and made out someone hurrying down the street.

She was a fool. She should have been more careful. But

who would look up at the roof to see a girl running through the sky?

One leap, it seemed hardly more than a small step, and Livy was clambering over the parapet of the White Tower.

"Did you miss me?" She laughed as she put her hand out to the Sentinel's broken carved wing. It was ridiculous to talk to a piece of stone this way, but she couldn't shake off the feeling that it would be rude to ignore that stern, unchanging face.

She settled down under the broken wing, reached into her backpack for her vocabulary book, and looked at the list of French words she still had to learn.

The book with the seagull on the cover had fallen out and she picked it up. She flicked through the pages, blurry photographs of seagulls against leaden skies. A page must have come loose, and a gust of wind caught it and it flapped across the roof. Livy jumped up and put her foot on it, then bent down to pick it up.

The paper was thicker and coarser than the smooth pages of the book. The ink was a faded brown and the letters were written in such curls and flourishes that it was at first hard to read what was written there.

"Rise, ye children of golde," Livy whispered. Her skin itched on the inside as her words were taken away by the breeze, like smoke. The next few words had been scratched out. "Something something bloode is lighter than an Angell's wing," she read.

How had this piece of paper gotten trapped in a book about seagulls? And why would such words have such an effect on her? As she had read those words, she had felt as if she could rise effortlessly into the air—in fact, she was having to clutch onto the Sentinel's stone feet to keep herself on the roof.

"What are you doing here?"

Livy—intent on trying to keep herself heavy enough not to float away—was so startled by the voice that she looked up into the Sentinel's face. Had he spoken?

"I asked you what you're doing here!"

The boy with the green eyes stood in front of her.

Livy hastily closed the book with the paper inside. She felt guilty, somehow, although she hadn't been doing anything wrong.

"Nothing!" she blurted out. "Just reading."

But of course, now that he was standing just feet away from her, she knew that she had not been remotely interested in learning French vocabulary on the roof. She had wanted to see him all along.

She wrinkled her nose as that strange smell of burnt metal surrounded her. She felt light-headed.

The boy stepped closer. "I told you to stay away from here. You're not wanted."

As he spoke, Livy heard again his strange accent, the words clipped and almost swallowed. The wind took hold of his coat and it flapped around him like a crow's ragged wing. The gold flecks in his eyes flared.

"I don't have to do what you say!" Livy's voice struck the air like a lighted match. "I can come up here whenever I like and you can't do anything to stop me!"

"Can't I?" the boy said. "You'd better not test me!"

He was taller than her, it was true, but painfully thin. His skin, luminous as the moon, was drawn tight over his cheekbones, and his narrow shoulders looked as if they could scarcely bear the weight of his coat.

Seeing how frail he was, Livy felt braver. "You don't scare me."

The boy looked shocked. "I'm not trying to scare you. I'm warning you. Stay away. Don't come near me." He closed his eyes, looking pained. "It's all beginning again. I can feel it in my blood . . ." He clutched at his temples.

"Are you OK?" She put out her hand.

"Get away! It's all happening because of *you!*"

He snatched up the book that she had been reading, that stray piece of paper tucked inside. "Keep your books and your ideas away from here!" He flung the book into the air and it seemed to hover for a second before it fell into the Court of Sentinels below.

"Hey!" Livy yelled. "You've got no right to throw my things around!" She scrambled to her feet and looked over the parapet. The book had fallen open and the pages were blowing mournfully back and forth in the wind. The strange handwritten paper was nowhere to be seen.

"These books will cause a fever in your brain," the boy cried, "and then you will start it all again!"

"I . . . I don't know what you're talking about. I won't start anything. I promise."

"You're a Burgess. Your promises are worthless! You won't be able to stop yourself!" He leaned in closer. "*Tempus fugit*," he hissed.

Livy felt the lead tremble beneath her feet. A door had been slammed shut somewhere deep in the tower. She felt the bitter air stir around her and heard the flapping of a bird's wings as it took to the sky.

"Get away," the boy's voice whispered in her ear. "There's bad blood between you and me."

She turned. The boy had gone. Escaped across the roof.

"Hello?" she called into the night. "Where are you?" She once again felt her anger rise. "You can't just throw my book off the roof and disappear!" She screwed up her eyes to try and focus on the roof of Temple College. Where had he run to? "Come back here!"

No answer.

Livy was aware of how cold it was on the roof; the wind had picked up and found its way through her clothes, chilling her bones. She shivered and her teeth chattered. But her body's tremors were not only due to the cold—the boy's words had affected her in a way that she couldn't understand.

"He can't tell me to stay away," Livy said to the Sentinel, as if the stone head might turn and agree with her. She sat back down as if she could once more feel that the roof was hers. But Livy no longer felt safe. She felt that the night was trying to push her off the White Tower. The clouds reared up like vast white waves and she had the impression that they might roll toward her and crush her. Livy wrapped her arms around her knees and closed her eyes. She would not move.

"Ralph?" It was a child's voice. "I'm scared."

Livy opened her eyes. "Who's there?"

She could see shadows on the parapet, a row of seven children, standing with their arms in front of them. One, much taller, was trying to shake off a long, ragged coat and the small boy next to him tugged anxiously at the sleeve of the coat. "Wait, can't you?" he whispered to the younger child.

"But is it time?" The voice was small and frightened.

It's all beginning again. I can feel it in my blood.

Those were the boy's words. But he was no longer there,

and now neither were the children—all that was left was a trembling impression in the air.

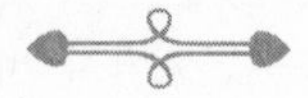

Livy didn't want to admit to herself that she was seeing things. That would mean that her situation had become very serious indeed. Her therapist had told her that "feeling odd" was all to be expected as Livy got over Mahalia's death but had said nothing about seeing people who didn't exist, who *couldn't* exist. She had allowed things to get out of hand, she had to get back to her room and not let the night air excite her.

So, telling herself that she was going to go calmly back to her room and finish her homework, Livy picked up her backpack and clambered over the parapet. But her body was not so easily tricked; her legs felt weak and her hands were shaking. The air itself had changed; she couldn't move through the night with the same careless confidence. Instead she felt as if she had to push her way through the air around her—it had become thick and heavy. How stupid had she been to think that she could climb on the roof and not come to any harm? The boy was right. She should not have gone.

Then she heard his whispered words again, but so clearly that they could have been spoken into her ear. She turned her head.

There's bad blood between you and me.

"It makes no sense!" she shouted. But in that instant, she felt no more solid than smoke. She closed her eyes, pushed herself away from the chimneystack, and slid down the tiles.

In a state of panic, she opened her eyes. The roof was running out, the ground approaching too quickly. She caught hold of the frame of her open window just in time and, panting, swung her legs over the sill.

Livy sat there for a second, as she tried to calm herself. She felt herself settle, as if her body were becoming more solid. Then she jumped down and threw herself on her bed, enjoying her body becoming gradually heavier, like when she let the water out of the bath.

Livy was startled by the window blowing shut. She got up and fastened it tight, pressing her forehead against the cold glass as she stared across at the Sentinel. Where was the boy? She shivered as she thought how he had stood only feet away from her, the air wrapping itself around them, trapping that strange bitter scent of smoke. Livy lifted her arm and sniffed the jacket of her blazer, inhaling the smell. She drew her hair across her mouth and tasted it. But there had been no fire on the roof, so how was she drenched in that bitter scent?

CHAPTER SIXTEEN

"I can't go to school. I have a headache."

Livy's mother sat on the edge of the bed and put her hand to Livy's forehead. "No temperature, so you have to go."

"But I feel awful!" Livy blurted out. She wanted her mother to stop looking at her with that concerned face, and she wanted to be alone in her room so that she could think about what had happened on the roof.

"You know the rules." Her mother sounded too reasonable. "Unless you've been sick or you have a fever, you have to go to school. You promised me, Livy. You've missed enough time as it is because I let you stay off for so long when you were so undone over Mahalia. But I'm not being kind to you if I let you start avoiding school now. Otherwise, before we know it, we'll be back to how it was when you refused to go to school and all you did was lie around on the sofa all day. I realize now that it wasn't good for you; you should have been with your other friends." Her mother sounded firm, as if she really meant what she said and Livy would be going to school.

"But I'm ill!" Livy hit the bedclothes with her fist in frustration.

"If you've got the energy to shout at me, then you've got the energy to get up and go to school." Her mother stood up. "Dressed and downstairs in ten minutes, Livy. I mean it."

As Livy walked as slowly as possible down the stairs, having dawdled as long as she dared getting dressed, her mind spiraled around the strange occurrences of the night before.

"I won't tell Mommy." Tom was standing in his bedroom doorway, staring at her intently.

"Won't tell her what?" Livy pulled her hair back into a ponytail.

"It's a secret."

"Yeah, whatever, Tom," she said, going into the bathroom to brush her teeth.

Tom appeared in the doorway. "Will you take me with you?"

Livy laughed. "To school? They don't have little children like you at Temple College."

Tom shook his head. "Not *there*."

"Where?"

"Will you take me to the sky? I won't tell."

A trembling image of a boy clutching at a dark sleeve. Livy gasped and shook her head to free herself of that troubling scene.

"The sky's no place for you, Tom," she snapped. "It's no place for anyone, only birds."

"And Count Zacha," Tom said, his eyes wide. "He chases pigeons. I want to chase them too." He put his arms out and tilted his body to get past her. "Pyoo-pyoo . . ." he cried, mimicking the sound of his Warrior Copter as he pretended to fly toward the stairs. "Watch out pigeons! I'll get you for my pie!"

The morning dragged, the time crawled. Livy watched every clock in Temple College and checked her phone frequently to see how much longer it would be until she could climb out of her window and onto the roof.

"Are you feeling OK?" Celia asked as Livy pushed her uneaten lunch around her plate. "You seem distracted."

Livy's skin burned and itched; she felt as if her blood was too hot inside her veins. She looked up to see another portrait of Peter Burgess staring down at her. He looked older and sadder in this painting—his dark eyes could have been holes cut in the canvas—and he held a full white rose in his hand. She had never noticed before, but there was a large drop of crimson blood on one of the petals.

The boy on the roof, Livy thought for the hundredth time that day. What was this bad blood between them? And what could be starting again? But the more troubling question was: How could it have anything to do with her?

"Livy?" Celia nudged her. "What's up?"

Livy shrugged. The effort of speaking was almost unbearable. "Headache."

"Do you want me to take you to the school nurse? She gives you chocolate and you can lie down on the couch in her office."

Livy shook her head.

"Can I have your dessert?" Martha asked, not waiting for a reply as she stuck her spoon into the crumble. "If you're not going to eat it. It's Thursday. I can have dessert on a Thursday."

Livy pushed the tray toward her. "Be my guest."

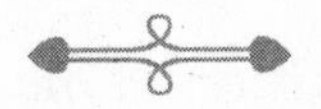

Livy stood on her own in the Court of Sentinels. Celia had left to go to one of her many clubs. Today's was a "Young

Women in Science" study group with Dr. Smythe. Martha and Amy, who had promised to look after Livy, were standing a few feet away, whispering to each other as they looked intently at Martha's phone.

Livy saw Alex disappear into the archway that led to the cloisters. She followed him.

"Where's she going?" Livy heard Amy ask Martha.

"To be boring somewhere else."

Livy saw Alex staring up at a blue plaque on the wall with gold lettering. She remembered that Celia had told her that it held the names of the poor children that Master Burgess had brought to Temple College and educated at his own expense. It was an odd thing to be looking at so intently.

"What's so interesting?" Livy said.

"Do you see anything odd?" Alex said, not taking his eyes from the dull gold letters and seemingly not surprised that she should be standing next to him.

Livy looked up. "Hugh Foxe, Ezra Maskelyne." She turned to Alex. "Is that who the house is named after?"

"His son," Alex nodded. "Something big in astronomy."

"Josiah Phelps," Livy continued. "They had pretty weird names back then."

"Not the names," Alex said, sounding irritated. "Look at the spaces between them." He reached up. "There's a gap here," he whispered, tapping his finger on the board. "As if someone's name has been removed."

Livy looked up. She risked standing on her tiptoes, even though that sensation of lifting her heels off the floor was dangerous. She put her finger to the place where another coat of blue paint had been applied.

"*Something* happened to that boy," Alex said thoughtfully. "Why else would his name be removed?"

"Perhaps he just left the school."

Alex shook his head. "You wouldn't have to paint out his name. I think something more serious happened and it was covered up. This is as if someone had tried to erase not just the boy's name, but his existence."

"Why do you care so much?" Although Livy, too, felt curious.

"I told you. I'm interested in the history of Temple College—all the stained-glass windows and the paintings. But when I asked Mr. Hopkins why Peter Burgess put seven Sentinels on the roof, he just said, 'Tempus fugit' and 'Only a real Burgess would know.' What sort of answer is that? Especially as it is now clear that you don't know anything! But he seemed frightened, too, as if there was something he couldn't say."

Lunch break was almost over and they walked slowly back into the Court of Sentinels. Alex looked up at the roof. "See?" he said. "How many can you count?"

"There are seven," Livy said. "I don't need to count them."

"And yet there are only six names on the board," Alex mused.

"Seven sentinels, six scholars . . ." Livy was trying to remember something. "Dr. Smythe said perhaps it cost more to educate a boy than to have a Sentinel carved. Perhaps Master Burgess was going to pick another child, but he ran out of money."

"Was this something else she said at your interview?" Alex looked unimpressed. "That you can't really remember?"

Livy's attention was distracted by seeing Celia chatting animatedly to Amy and Martha. All three girls stopped and stared as Joe Molyns walked past. He halted a few feet away, unaware of his audience.

Alex said, puzzled, "Why does Celia bother with those two?"

"It's a girl thing," Livy said. "You wouldn't understand."

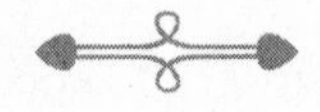

Livy was thinking about Celia and Joe as she turned into Leaden Lane. Would he really be more interested in Martha or Amy?

"A penny for your thoughts, Miss Burgess?"

Mr. Hopkins, looking tired and unkempt, as if he had spent the night under a bridge or sleeping on a bench, had tapped her on the shoulder. His hat was squashed, as though he had sat on it.

"Oh, it's nothing," Livy explained. "I was just thinking about some people at school." She smiled. She felt awkward that this poor man had been thrown out of his house and now was clearly in need of somewhere decent to sleep.

"Not Dr. Smythe?" Mr. Hopkins winced.

"No."

"A relief, Miss Burgess."

Anxious to get away from the subject of Dr. Smythe and how she had sacked Mr. Hopkins and given his job and house to Livy's dad, Livy asked the first thing that came into her head. "Could I ask you a question?"

"Of course. I'd be delighted to help you. If I can. Time was when I was being asked questions all day long. There were plenty of curious minds at Temple College." His eyes glinted.

"Why are there seven Sentinels on the roof? You told a friend of mine that only a real Burgess would know."

"Do you mean Alex? The clever Russian boy?"

Livy nodded.

"Perhaps you are not meant to know . . . yet . . ." The

man frowned. “A word of warning, Miss Burgess.” He looked over his shoulder as if he expected they might be overheard. “Don’t let Dr. Smythe know of your interest in these matters.”

“Why?”

He shrugged his shoulders inside his crumpled coat. “It will only cause trouble.”

“But the missing boy?” Livy asked.

The man looked surprised. His eyes darted toward Temple College. “What boy?”

“Everyone talks of the six boys that Peter Burgess brought to Temple College—”

“And there are six names on the board,” Mr. Hopkins interrupted her. “Abel Carter, Hugh Foxe, Ezra Maskelyne, Edmund Moore, Josiah Phelps, and George Philips.”

“There wasn’t one more?”

“Why, no!”

“But underneath Josiah Phelps. There’s a space where a name could go. It’s been painted over.”

Mr. Hopkins shook his head. “Well, so far as I know, there were only six children.” The man shivered as if he were cold. “I don’t suppose that you could spare some change for a cup of tea?” He coughed. “It’s turned very cold of late.”

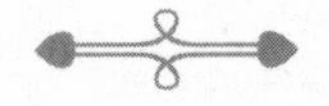

Livy stared out her window at the Sentinel with the broken wing. The seventh Sentinel on the roof. No. It was silly. Alex had gotten her mind racing. Mr. Hopkins had been quite clear. There were only six boys. She thought about Alex and the way his face had lit up as he looked at the scholars' board. He had made her think there might actually be a mystery!

She wondered what Mahalia would have said if she had been there.

Livy looked up at the sky. The winter was already here, heavy and cold. All those days that Mahalia had not seen.

"Where are you?" she whispered to a bright star above the Sentinel's head. "Can you see me? No! Don't look over there. I've moved. I'm here. I'm hanging out of the window to make it easier for you. Look, I'm waving to you."

She put her arm down then, feeling slightly foolish. Her chest felt tight.

"I'm in a muddle, Mahalia," she said, although whether she was speaking to her friend or herself, she didn't really know. "I don't know what I think about anything anymore. Or how I feel. Except that I feel strange. I wish you could come back and talk to me. Let me know that you are safe. I gave Jerron your glass heart . . ."

But she didn't want to say any more about that afternoon. The boy hadn't even known Mahalia's name.

"I'm at this new school now. With new people. Maybe you saw Martha and Amy. They're the shiniest shiny girls ever. But Celia is nice. You'd like her, I think. She's crazy about a boy named Joe. But she won't talk to him. She's not brave like you."

Livy felt her throat go dry. She chewed her lip for a moment.

"And there's this other boy named Alex. He's really into history. He thinks there's a mystery at the school. He thinks a boy disappeared. It was hundreds of years ago, when the school was new. Except Mr. Hopkins—he's the old librarian, my dad took his job, long story—says the boy was never there in the first place . . ." She was running on. "Sorry if I'm boring you . . . And then there's . . ."

How could she explain how she had climbed onto the roof?

Livy swung her legs out of the window. "Maybe I'll just show you. Watch me, Mahalia . . ."

CHAPTER SEVENTEEN

Livy immediately felt lighter, as if the confusion and heaviness of the day was no longer a burden.

"Abel Carter, Hugh Foxe," she whispered. "Ezra Maskelyne, Edmund Moore, Josiah Phelps, George Philips . . ."

The six names had the quality of a poem, she thought. Or a spell.

"Can you see me, Mahalia?" she said. "Look how fast I am! I'm not scared. I'm brave. Like you."

She stretched her hand out toward the Sentinel and thought that she saw the great wings shudder and move to reveal . . . the boy! He was standing on the parapet, looking down into the Court of Sentinels.

"Hey!" she cried.

The boy turned, his coat flapping in the wind. Livy increased her pace.

"Can I talk to you?"

The boy looked angry. "Get away!" he yelled.

"But I want to talk to you! I want to tell you that—"

"Is it gold you want? Like the last Burgess? Do you want to be rich beyond measure?"

"No!" Livy cried. The boy must be disturbed to be shouting like that.

"A child will suffer!" he said, his face contorted with anger. "I won't help you! I won't get the leeches!" He turned away and raised his arms as if he were about to dive into a swimming pool.

Livy halted. "Leeches?" But the strangeness of his speech was soon blown away as the boy raised his heels off the stone. He closed his eyes, tipped forward. "No!" she cried out, but he seemed to hover there, on the very edge of the roof, for longer than was possible. The minutes swelled and expanded. How was he able to hang in the air for so long?

"Stop!" Livy yelled, running toward him again.

The boy looked over his shoulder. His eyes flashed.

And then he jumped.

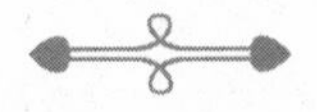

Livy stopped. What had she seen? The boy had been there one minute and gone the next. "He's all right, he's all right, he's all right," she told herself as she climbed up onto the roof. But her pulse was racing and her palms were so slippery that she nearly fell back onto the roof of the house below.

She scrambled over the parapet and was in such a state that she thought that she felt the Sentinel's broken wing shiver as she touched it. She felt the lead beneath her feet shake—a heavy door had been slammed deep in the tower. She heard footsteps running across the Court of Sentinels. *Is it him?* Blood pounding in her head, she forced herself to look over the parapet at whatever might be below.

But there was no body lying broken on the flagstones and whoever the footsteps had belonged to had disappeared into the deep shadows cast by the moon.

"Where are you?"

As Livy stared down, she noticed that the window in the tower just beneath her looked as if it had been pushed open. Had the boy done that? Had he climbed down? There was no other way he could have gone. There was a solid-looking drainpipe and, if she could hold on to it, she might be able to reach the window. Really, it wasn't such a difficult thing to do.

She swung her legs over the parapet, reached across to grasp the cold metal drainpipe, and then, a moment later, she had jumped across the gap and was standing on the curved stone window ledge, pulling the mullioned glass farther open. But here she was stopped—the shutter was jammed. She dug her fingers between the wooden panels. When the wood gave, her heart leapt as she almost toppled back. She grabbed at the window frame just in time.

She let her breathing settle before she pushed at the heavy shutter. It opened with a creak as if it were complaining at being moved.

Livy climbed inside; the window was so small that she had to bend and squeeze and draw her legs to her chest before she could drop down onto the floor.

Her eyes slowly adjusted to the gloom.

CHAPTER EIGHTEEN

Livy was standing in a small round room with a low ceiling.

"Hello?" she called out.

There was no reply. She went to the door and rattled the handle. It was locked. Seeing logs burning in a carved stone fireplace and realizing that her hands were cold, Livy stepped forward. The warmth from the flames felt so delightful that she flopped down into the depths of a saggy, velvet-covered armchair. By her elbow was a low table on which someone had placed a pewter jug, a horn beaker, and a plate of small frosted cookies.

Suddenly ravenous, Livy's hand hovered over the cookies. Would anyone notice? I'll just take a couple, she told herself, rearranging the others to make her theft less obvious. They tasted of butter and brown sugar and cinnamon. She poured a drink into the beaker and sipped at the elderflower cordial, Mahalia's favorite.

Feeling revived, Livy looked around. "What a strange little room," she said to herself. Could this be where the boy lived? Perhaps he had climbed down here each time he had disappeared so swiftly. But it was a strange sort of room for a boy to live in. There was a round mirror on the wall, but when Livy stood up to look into it, the mirror did not show her reflection, remaining blacker than the night. There were piles of crystals on tables and a large cupboard that, when opened, revealed row upon row of slim drawers. Livy pulled at one and inside found trays of feathers, all neatly labeled.

She turned the handle on the door. It was locked, which meant that she would have to leave by the same way she had gotten in. But why would the boy lock the door? Was there something of value in the room? Something more precious than a tray of feathers?

There were scratches on the doorframe and she reached out to trace them. They must have been old because they were blurred and dark, as if they had been drawn in charcoal. "RS," she breathed. They meant nothing.

Unable to stop herself, she took another cookie. But, thinking that perhaps this was the boy's food that she was eating, she put the cookie back. She wanted to think of him sitting here in front of the fire surrounded by the astrological charts that lined the walls. He had always looked so cold and hungry.

Perhaps these were his books on the bookshelf.

She picked up a tiny leather-bound volume. *The Weight of an Angel's Wing,* she read in the minuscule gilt lettering on the spine, *By a Scholar of Temple College.* She opened the book carefully and gasped at the intricate ink drawings of an angel flying through the night sky, hair curled around its noble face and wearing a long gown like her Sentinel.

"The wingspan of an Angel is the length of seven Celestial Kingdoms," Livy read, "and its weight is but that of a Rose Petal."

It was so odd. Temple College had a centuries-old reputation for educating scientists. In fact, Dr. Smythe had given an assembly that morning where she had talked about a famous physicist who had been a Templar. Livy had not listened, preferring instead to look up at the remains of the stained-glass window, now held together with sheets of plastic. But she remembered Dr. Smythe explaining that the real discovery that had been made at Temple College was you should believe only what you could see with your own eyes.

"Unlike other places of learning, four hundred years ago, there was no magic at Temple College," Dr. Smythe had declared. "Only science."

And yet here was a book written by one of the scholars of Temple College that was not remotely scientific, that was all about angels and celestial kingdoms, imaginary things that could never be seen.

Livy put another log on the fire and, as the sparks

flew, she noticed a low bench on which several flasks and glass beakers had been set out. Was the boy engaged in some sort of experiment? She thought of the peculiar burning smell that always seemed to surround him. On the bench was another book, slim and bound in red leather. *On Alchemie* was stamped in faded gold letters on the cover.

On the first page was a woodcut of a rose. It had been pierced with a lance and there was a single drop of blood that had been colored in bright red ink. Roses like this were all around Temple College, repeated so often that no one took any notice of them. Like those words, *tempus fugit,* no one really knew what they meant.

Livy turned the page. The words seemed to tremble as she read them: "To make a Powder of Alteration that will heal and purify the Bloode." Below the title was a picture of flasks and beakers set out exactly as they were on the bench.

Is this what the boy was studying? Could he be trying to solve the problem of impure blood, blood that did not behave as it should? Such a powder of alteration would have been something that would have saved Mahalia. Could it stop Livy's pulse from racing and get rid of this itching, burning sensation under her skin? She felt an answering flare in her veins, as if her blood agreed. Livy picked up a flask filled with strange gray dust. She shook it and the dust clung to the sides of the flask. She thought of her science paper—a cure for leukemia—and how Dr. Smythe had encouraged her. Could she really make a powder that would calm her blood? Was it too much to imagine that this old, timeworn book, written when medicine was more magic than science, contained a long-overlooked secret that only she could understand?

But then she remembered Alex. *Twelve-year-olds don't find cures for anything.*

Livy put the flask down, her mood deflated. It couldn't happen and was, in any case, too late for Mahalia . . .

But then, why had the boy—for this must be his room—set out these flasks and beakers and powders and liquids like this, just as they were shown in the book? She read and reread the book, trying to understand what she was to do. The words read like a fairy story of Red Kings and White Queens . . . red and white. Red blood, of course, was good, but white blood . . .

Livy thought about the thin tube—a cannula—that had been in stuck into the back of Mahalia's hand when she first went into the hospital. This was so the nurses could take vial after vial of her blood. Mahalia didn't complain, but she did say that it made her vein sore. Peter Burgess, according to Dr. Smythe, had used leeches to take blood for his experiments. She shuddered. Had his young patients been as calm as Mahalia? Or had they cried out in alarm and squirmed as the creatures were put on their skin? But perhaps leeches weren't actually painful. Perhaps they tickled, like when she and Mahalia had lain in the grass in the park, talking and talking, and the ants had crawled over them. The paintings of Master Burgess did not make him look like a cruel man.

A sliver of gray light slipped onto the floor. The sun had come up!

Livy put the book back on the bookshelf, ate just one more cookie, and climbed out the window.

She didn't feel tired. Instead she felt as if she had enjoyed the longest sleep and was only now waking up. She lay full-length on the lead-covered roof and stared up at the Sentinel's face above her. It must have been cold because her breath floated out on a cloud, but she felt warm, as if the flame from the candle in the little room was now burning inside her.

She had jumped down onto the roof behind the White Tower when she heard a voice behind her.

"Rise, ye children of golde!"

She turned. A man wearing a long black cloak was standing on the roof, his arms outstretched as if he would pull the sun up above the horizon and set it in the sky above him. A group of children huddled together.

"Hey!" Livy called out. "Be careful."

But they couldn't have heard her.

Was she seeing things? The light had a peculiar quality to it, shivering and humming. The figures were not solid; she had to strain her eyes to hold the picture clearly. The boys were dressed strangely, wearing loose thin smocks. They clung together, their thin little bodies shivering in the morning chill. One could not have been much older than Tom. He turned his head toward Livy.

"Be careful!" she cried out. The boy was so little and too close to the edge.

"I'm so hungry," he whispered, his lips chapped. "I could eat the heavens like a pie."

Livy could see the last morning stars twinkling through the boy; he was no more solid than the thinnest wisp of cloud.

A siren blared in the street below. The air shook, and emptied itself.

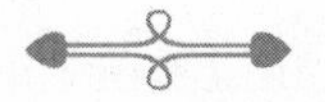

It was just a waking dream, she told herself as she climbed carefully over the tiles back down to her room, an illusion brought on by spending all night awake in the tower trying to find a cure for bad blood. And this had gotten mixed up, like the filings swirling in the flask, with Alex and his crazy ideas about the scholars that Master Burgess had brought to the school. Yes. That was what it was. Her imagination was making pictures out of nothing.

Livy lifted a lock of her hair to her nose. It smelled of smoke. So did her school sweater. She remembered her sessions with the therapist her mother had sent her to during those long, dragging summer weeks after Mahalia had died.

"There will be things your parents can't understand about what you are experiencing," the woman had said. "And even if you tell them, they won't be able to help you . . ."

The words had made Livy feel very small and alone. She had always had someone to talk to before. But now the secrets were piling up and she had no one to tell about the way she felt in her body, those strange sensations where her blood seemed to burn in her veins, and the way her heels would rise up off the floor. She couldn't tell anyone about her impulse to climb out the window and onto the roof. And the boy who had disappeared into the night. She definitely couldn't tell anyone about the boy . . .

But she had read about a powder of alteration that would heal and purify blood. And she would make a powder of alteration that, if it was too late for Mahalia, would alter *her,* would get rid of these sensations, these secrets, these stupid visions, and make her feel like herself, her real self, again.

"Did you see him?"

It was Tom. He had climbed onto Livy's windowsill and was leaning right out, craning his little head to look up at her.

"Tom," Livy said as calmly as she could. "I want you to climb back down."

Tom didn't seem to care that he was just inches from peril.

"But did you see Count Zacha?" Tom was peering past Livy at the sky and the Sentinel.

Livy slid as quickly as she dared down to her window and almost pushed Tom off the windowsill. "Don't ever climb up here again, do you hear me?" she said, her pulse hammering.

Tom narrowed his eyes. "Why can you climb out of the window and not me?"

Livy looked at him. His hair was ruffled and he rubbed his fat-lidded eyes. What should she say?

"You're tired, Tom," she whispered into his ear as she picked him up. "I don't think you did see me climb in through the window. I think that you are having a dream."

Tom put his head on Livy's shoulder.

"You are going to wake up later and you will be all warm and cozy in your bed," Livy went on as she carried him down the stairs.

"But I don't think this is a dream." Tom pulled his

head back and looked at Livy suspiciously. "I think I am awake. Look!" And he opened his eyes as wide as possible.

"I'm not so sure, Tom," Livy whispered as she put her little brother down on his bed. "Dreams can feel very real."

She tucked his quilt around his squat body and stroked his hair.

Tom yawned. His eyelids fluttered closed for a moment. "I am lying on a cloud," he said.

"Is it soft?" Livy said.

"It is floaty," Tom whispered and sucked his thumb.

Livy sat with him until his breathing was regular and his thumb fell out of his mouth.

CHAPTER NINETEEN

Martha and Amy were up to something, Livy could see. They whispered and giggled all through the first lesson with more drama than usual.

As they left the classroom, Livy got a notification on her phone. She opened it to see a little bit of shaky film.

"What's that?" Celia asked, craning her head to see the screen.

"Nothing!" Livy slipped her phone back in her pocket. She wouldn't give Martha or Amy the satisfaction of knowing that she had seen it.

But—of course—Celia had been sent the same notification. Livy wanted to tell her to put her phone away, but that would only make it worse. Martha and Amy would love the drama. Livy knew that Celia was now looking at that same film, which started with blurry, moving gray blazers. The blazers would part and there would be a glimpse of Celia, staring into the distance with the words "Celia Jones ♥ Joe Molyns" below her rapt expression. Whoever had been secretly filming Celia then moved the phone to show what she was staring at—Joe Molyns standing with his back to her, oblivious of her adoration. "#Unrequited" now covered the screen, pulsing in bright fluorescent green as a cartoon tear splashed onto the ground.

"Oh," Celia said quietly as she put her phone away.

"Celia! Did you see this?" Amy gasped, waving her phone.

"Who could have done such a mean thing?" Martha said, a look of fake concern on her face.

Others in the group waiting to go into the next class were looking at their phones and whispering, turning to stare at Celia.

"It's just too cruel." Amy's eyes glittered. "Don't cry, Celia."

"She's not crying," Livy said as she pulled Celia into the classroom.

"I'll never live it down." Celia closed her eyes.

"Just delete it."

"But what happens if . . . if . . . Joe Molyns sees it?" She sank into a chair and put her hand to a flushed cheek. "Tell me, do I really look that *obvious*?"

"I doubt he'll see it. It's only been sent to our class."

Celia groaned. "What am I going to do?"

"Nothing."

"What?" Celia looked startled.

"You're going to do nothing. You're not going to give them the pleasure of knowing that they've upset you. If they can't upset you, they can't win."

"But who could have done such a thing?"

"You really don't know?"

Celia's mouth twitched. "But they wouldn't."

"They have."

"But they're my friends."

"Look, we're sorry." Livy and Celia turned to see Martha and Amy standing in the doorway. Martha made a face. "Don't be mad, Celia. It was just a little joke, a bit of fun."

"Quite harmless," Amy added.

"Is Celia laughing?" Livy snapped.

"But it was just a *little* bit funny," Martha explained as if Livy were stupid. "With the hashtag and the tear . . ." She pulled an exaggerated sad face.

"How? How is it funny for Celia?"

Martha's mouth twitched. "Well, Livy, we can't expect *you* to understand. You don't know how things work around here. You're new. And . . . and . . . *different*."

"That bag," Amy cut in. "I mean . . ." She rolled her eyes.

"But Celia's one of *us.* She understands our little jokes," Martha continued. "She knows that we find other people *amusing.*" Martha stared at Celia, who looked down at the desk. "Remember, Celia? Who we found funny yesterday?"

"No," Celia said. "No, I don't remember. And even if I did, I didn't like it. I didn't agree with what you were saying. You were being mean. And unfair."

"Well, if you're going to get all *weird* about it." Martha flicked her hair.

"Good luck with your new best friend—I mean your *leech.*" Amy smirked and they retreated to the other side of the classroom as Mr. Bowen came in.

"I'm sorry," Celia whispered to Livy as Mr. Bowen started handing out worksheets. "They were a bit mean about you yesterday and I didn't stick up for you hard enough."

Livy knew how it felt not to stick up for someone. When the shiny girls at her old school had laughed about Mahalia being too tired to do PE, Livy had said nothing just to avoid being turned on herself. A week later, Mahalia had been in hospital.

"But you stood up for me," Celia went on. "Thanks." And she squeezed Livy's arm.

"What happened?" Alex, late as always, threw his bag under the desk and slumped into the seat behind them. "You two look *intense.*"

"Girl stuff," Livy explained.

"Mean girl stuff," Alex corrected her. "Let me guess—Martha and Amy."

Celia looked flustered. "Let's not talk about it."

"You got upset about that stupid film?"

"It was humiliating, Alex," Celia muttered.

"Not really," Alex said. "Those two are such idiots. They're the ones who should feel humiliated."

Celia looked less sure.

"Why not tell Mr. Bowen? Give them a scare!"

"Because Martha and Amy will love the drama." Celia sighed. "What am I going to do?" She glanced across the classroom. "I've got art club with them after lunch."

"Come to chess club instead!" Alex smiled. "You can come, too, Livy."

"Chess?" Celia groaned. "Is this what my life has become?"

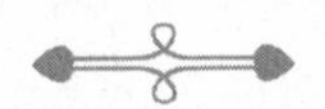

Livy did not admit when she climbed onto the roof that night that she was hoping to see the boy. If she hesitated before she swung her legs over the parapet to clutch at the drainpipe and make the leap to the window, she told herself that it was because the night was clear and cold and that she was looking at the stars. Despite the glow over the city, she could clearly see the pole star above her. "I won't be disappointed," she said to herself, "if, when I push open the shutters, the room is empty."

Of course it was empty, but when she jumped down into the quiet room, she had the impression that someone had only just left. The logs had not been alight for long and the room was still cold.

She took a cinnamon cookie, just one, in case the boy should return and feel hungry.

"I had a friend," she whispered to herself, practicing what she would say if the door opened and the boy stepped inside. That scowl on his face would melt away as she explained to him what she was doing. "She was my best friend. We did everything together. But then she got ill. She had a problem with her blood. Did you know that Peter Burgess called blood a 'living force'?"

No, she shouldn't mention Peter Burgess to the boy—that would bring the scowl back. She took another cookie while she considered what she should say. "My friend is on her own now," she said, filling the empty air with a trembling image of the boy. She made the image tilt his head as if he were listening more intently. "Mahalia was so funny. She would even make *you* laugh! We told each other everything. We made a promise never to have any secrets and now, every day that she's not here, I'm breaking that promise." Livy closed her eyes. "She must be so lonely because she had to leave everyone behind." She swallowed. "Who can she talk to now?"

The boy's imagined face softened. She had made him feel sorry for Mahalia. Livy opened her eyes. She made him ask her how long Mahalia had been alone for.

With a catch in her voice, Livy whispered back, "Five months. That's a long time—too long for Mahalia."

"And it's only the beginning," the imagined boy replied, shaking his head.

"Thing is—" Livy sniffed. This conversation was harder than she had thought it would be. "I'd like to make friends. Celia's nice and Alex, too. But it doesn't seem right for me to forget her and be happy with new people while she is so alone." The boy nodded as if he understood. "I think you are lonely, too," Livy whispered. Even though this was an imagined conversation and therefore the boy ought to behave as expected, he stepped away from her, turning to the door. She would have to speak fast to persuade him to stay. "I think that's why you shouted at me. You got me wrong. I'm not like how you say I am. I'm doing something good! I'm going to try and make this powder of alteration. From the book you left out for me, see?" She imagined him turning back to her now, and she raised the book to show the page to the empty air. "It says here that you can make a powder that will cure any illness in the blood. Oh, I know it won't help her, it's too late, but . . . perhaps I can help someone else. My own blood is doing really weird things and I know Alex said I couldn't cure anyone because I'm only twelve, but he can't know everything. I know it sounds silly, but just imagine . . . imagine if . . . I could really change someone's blood." Livy frowned. "Perhaps you want me to make this powder?" A thought struck her. "Is there something wrong with *your* blood, too? Perhaps you *need* it just as much as me?"

The logs settled in the fireplace, throwing up a shower of sparks. She was alone in the room.

But Livy felt different, as if after weeks of her body behaving in a way she couldn't understand and was unable to control, she might finally have a cure. She might, again, be able to rest in a body that felt like her own.

She settled down to read the book by the firelight, even more determined to make the powder.

There were no more stories of Red Kings and White Queens. Now she had come to the pages where whoever had written the book had set down his method. "Count 240 fine poudered grains and put to the flame." Livy, puzzled, looked at the illustrations again and came to the conclusion that she was to heat some of the metal filings over the candle. "Is that it?" She was perplexed; it didn't seem very scientific.

Livy inspected the equipment that had been left out for her on the workbench. Inside a smooth white stone bowl was a heap of dark metal filings. Would she really have to count them? She took up a pair of tiny tweezers and settled down to try and pick them up one by one and place them into the curve of a small wooden spoon. Sometime later, she carefully poured these "poudered grains" into the narrow neck of the flask.

She lit the candle; the flame danced and then settled. She swirled the metal filings around and then put the bottom of the flask to the flame. Livy watched, enraptured, as the gray metallic dust turned deep red and small pieces of a white substance appeared, like roses blooming on a lake of blood. This was the impurity, what the book had called "the dross," which needed to be repeatedly scraped away once the metal had cooled.

There was a moment when she burned her hand on the heated glass of the flask. As she blew on her skin, she did see how silly she was being. How could this metallic dust—that mere spoonful of metal filings—have the power to alter anything? But the thought quickly dissolved as she pulled her sleeve down over her hand to pick up the glass. She would do it again and again, all seven times as instructed. And tomorrow she would bring her mother's oven gloves from the kitchen to prevent further accidents. The candle flame flickered as if in agreement and Livy worked happily for hours—heating, cooling, scraping off the petals of dross—in the deep quiet of the room.

CHAPTER TWENTY

"You've just got to say hello to him, Celia. You can do that."

They were standing a few feet away from the convenience store. Joe Molyns was second in the line.

"I can't! I'll get nervous and blow it."

"But look, he's just standing there waiting to buy a drink. His friends aren't around. He's on his own. Just go."

"OK . . . Do I look OK?"

"You look fine. Better than fine. You look . . ."

Celia set off.

But just as Celia drew near, Joe turned and looked up the corridor as if he was looking for a friend. This spooked Celia. She swerved, flapped her arms in a strange little gesture, and turned around, her cheeks flaming. "Did he see me? Oh no. Oh, Livy. I couldn't do it. I just couldn't. What will he think?"

Another boy had joined Joe and they were talking amiably as Joe handed over his money and took the bottle of water.

"He won't think anything if you don't do something." Livy smiled. "You've got to be a bit braver."

Alex joined them just as Joe was leaving. "Do you have any money? I need sustenance!"

They shook their heads.

"Then what are you doing hanging around the store?" He put his hands to his stomach and mimed fainting. "I missed lunch because I was in the library. What's wrong with your dad, Livy?" He looked at Livy accusingly through narrow eyes. "He's so grumpy. I asked if I could go into the school archives and he nearly bit my head off."

"What do you want in the archives?" Livy asked. Celia was staring down the corridor, hoping for Joe to reappear.

"I wanted to find the list of the first pupils in Temple College. I thought that it would help me find out what happened to that boy. The seventh scholar."

"Are you still going on about that?" Celia said.

"Who told you?" Alex said, surprised.

"You did. You've been trying to get into the archives for weeks."

"I'm sorry about my dad," Livy said. "He's really stressed. He can't find the books Dr. Smythe is looking for."

"I thought she would be behind it," Alex said. "As she's behind most of what's odd around here."

They stepped out into the Court of Sentinels. Joe Molyns and his friends were kicking a soccer ball around. Martha and Amy were talking to one of the group.

"Urgh," muttered Alex.

"Joe's bound to pick one of them," Celia muttered. "Do you think if I changed my hair he would notice me? I could put a purple streak in."

Livy made a face. And then felt sad as she remembered how she and Mahalia had sprayed silver streaks in their hair last Halloween. But it was paint and they'd had to cut the streaks out.

"What is it with girls and their hair?" Alex grumbled. "You're either nice or you're not. What your hair looks like makes no difference! Honestly, you must think boys are stupid if you think a bit of purple is going to alter anything!"

"Are you going to try and say anything?" Livy whispered to Celia.

"After what just happened? I'm not brave enough."

"Just try."

"I can't. I just can't."

"Time to turn that frown upside down, Celia!" Alex laughed.

Livy was so surprised that she laughed, too.

"Come on," Alex said, tugging at Celia's sleeve. "I'm going to beat you at chess!"

"You wish!" Celia sniffed.

Later, as Livy put her key in the door, she thought about the room at the top of the White Tower and the powder of alteration. How long would she have to wait before she could go back there? Perhaps she could tell her mother that she had a headache, that she didn't need supper, and then she could go up to her room immediately. She assumed an "ill" expression as she opened the door. But her mother was oblivious, scarcely looking at her as she carried two mugs into the sitting room.

"Oh, Livy," she said. "You're back at last." She widened her eyes and tipped her head toward the door. "We've got a guest."

"I don't feel that great," Livy started to say, but her mother took no notice.

"Mr. Hopkins came to pay us a call. Isn't that nice? He used to do Dad's job." She lowered her voice so that the man in the sitting room wouldn't hear her. "I found him outside on the pavement a bit confused and upset." She raised her voice again. "Why don't you come and introduce yourself?"

Livy looked into the sitting room. Mr. Hopkins had taken off his hat and was perched on the sofa.

"I must say, Mrs. Burgess, you've made the house very cozy. I like all these cushions; it makes the sofa so comfy." He sighed. "A woman's touch." He looked broken and lonely and grateful for the tea her mother had made, wrapping his cold bony fingers around the warm mug.

"I am Tom!" Tom was standing on the back of the sofa. "I can fly—just like Count Zacha." He stuck his leg out into the air.

"Take no notice," Livy's mother whispered to Mr. Hopkins, rolling her eyes. "He's just showing off."

"Ah, the young." Mr. Hopkins smiled sadly. "Such imaginations! If only the world did not let us down as we get older. No, don't make him come down, Mrs. Burgess, let the boy dream."

Tom leapt forward and landed in a heap on the floor. *Thud.*

"Tom! Will you stop doing that!" Livy's mother said, sounding tired.

"He's got a bit of work to do on his landings." Mr. Hopkins chuckled indulgently.

Later, when Mr. Hopkins had gone, Livy finally convinced her mother that she wasn't feeling very well. She escaped from the kitchen, having been given an apple in case her pretend headache improved. But as she climbed the stairs, she heard her father come in, banging the front door closed. He was in a bad mood.

"Good day?" her mother called out.

"Urgh!" her father groaned. "That wretched man!"

"Who?"

Livy peered over the banister to see the tops of her parents' heads.

"Mr. Hopkins . . . Honestly, if I ever see that man . . ."

"Oh no, James, don't say that. He's a sweetheart."

"How would you know?"

There was a second's silence.

"Ros?"

"I think if you met him, James, you'd feel very differently."

"Would I?" Livy's father dropped his briefcase and kicked it under the hall table. "I somehow doubt that."

"Well, *I* feel sorry for him, James. He's had a hard time. No job. Left homeless. Dr. Smythe is the real villain of the piece. She's a witch, James. I'm not joking. She treated that poor man so badly."

"What makes you such an expert?"

Livy's mother must have whispered something that Livy couldn't hear.

"You did what?" Livy's father cried.

"I *had* to ask him in. He was standing outside in tears."

"Really? He's made my life a misery with his wretched filing, and you invite him in for tea? You'd better check where the teabags are, Ros! Mr. Hopkins will probably have put them in the freezer! Oh, and if you're looking for cookies, try the bathroom!"

"Oh, James, you're being unfair. He's just a lonely old man."

"Why do you think Dr. Smythe got rid of him? Because he was bad at his job."

"So she says!"

"Well anyway, if she hadn't, we would not be in this house and Livy would not be at Temple College. We could never have afforded that tuition without the scholarship that comes with my job. Or would you rather that he got his job back and we had to move?"

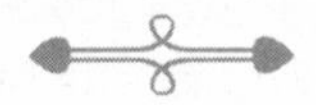

Livy pushed the idea away that they might leave the narrow house on Leaden Lane as she climbed the narrow stairs to her bedroom. She had work to do. Tonight she would test her powder of alteration.

The book had many warnings to be careful when handling the powder. It was powerful, and harmful, too, if touched by the wrong hands. It must be treated with care. Livy had taken the precaution of bringing her mother's best leather gloves from the drawer in the hall table because the oven gloves were too thick for such delicate work.

The powder was too strong to be used on herself without first being tested. On that, the book was clear. As she stood in her bedroom, her veins itching, she looked around for a suitable object to test her powder on. *Of course,* she thought as she reached out her hand and closed her fingers around the little box.

Moments later, she was in the room at the top of the White Tower. The fire was burning in the fireplace, the quiet of the room settled around her. She took a deep breath, the air faintly scented with metal and smoke. Blowing into her hands (the night climb had chilled her), she bent over to inspect her row of flasks. Her powder had bloomed again since the night before and she carefully scraped off the white petals of dross.

She took the small box out of her pocket and pushed it open to reveal the brown coin. She took it out and held it in the palm of her hand.

"Do you remember, Mahalia?" Livy pulled on her mother's gloves and then, numb to the metallic grains of powder and their effect, she sprinkled a pinch of gray powder onto the little disc. "This is your lucky penny. It never brought you any luck but I'm going to test my powder of alteration on it and perhaps it will become the luckiest penny ever." She had read in the book that the powder was so powerful that it could easily turn base metal into gold.

She held her breath, bending over the coin. "Come on," she whispered, tapping the edge of the coin with her gloved finger. "Do something."

The dull coin stubbornly refused.

The candlelight flickered and the fire stirred as a log settled, but the coin remained unchanged, unaltered in any way.

Livy stepped back from the desk, pulling off her gloves with her teeth. She felt sick. What was she doing? All this ridiculous counting of grains of metal and endless heating of the heavy flask in this stupid room! She looked around. She wouldn't be helping anyone with a sickness in their blood. Not Mahalia, not the boy, and certainly not herself. She scratched at the veins on her wrist. Stupid powder. Stupid coin. Stupid book. She snatched it, her veins on fire. "Stupid me!" She hurled the book toward the fire.

The book sat on the logs, the flames extinguished. "Good riddance," Livy muttered, "to bad rubbish!"

What had she hoped for? That the coin might become gold, as the book had boasted?

There was a small popping sound and the flames leapt up, green and blue and a deep rosy pink and swallowed the book. "Ha!" Livy turned away. "The flames can have you!"

Livy flipped the coin and watched as it spun up into the air that stirred, like a sigh. The flames leapt in the fireplace. Livy saw the glint of gold on the surface of the coin and gasped as the penny seemed to hang in the air . . .

It fell onto the workbench.

Dull and brown, a mere penny that had never brought any luck to anyone.

CHAPTER TWENTY-ONE

The next day, Celia, her face bright with excitement, ran toward Livy as she entered Temple College. But Livy didn't feel like hearing the news that Celia was clearly eager to share. She didn't want to be down here; her thoughts were still in the room in the White Tower and her failed experiment. Something had happened, she thought, when she had tossed the coin into the air. If only she could hold that image in her mind, she might see what had happened more clearly.

And because of that, Livy had not climbed back down to her bedroom straight away last night, but had lingered on the roof. She had lain on the chill gray lead and stared up at the sky. She had a strange sensation that Mahalia was behind one of those twinkling blue stars, hiding, and any moment, if Livy just kept watching, did not look away for a second, or even blink, Mahalia would step out, laughing, her dark eyes dancing with mischief.

"Did you think I had gone?" Livy had imagined her saying and felt a thrill as she remembered, so clearly that she had to catch her breath at the shock of it, Mahalia's singsong voice. "All along I've been just here, looking at you. I told you I'd always be your best friend. That's why I gave you my lucky penny when you came to see me in the hospital. It was to give you the luck I had no time for."

"All the teachers are in a state," Celia was saying now. Livy struggled to focus. "We all have to go to the Temple. Big announcement!" Celia frowned. "You have really dark circles under your eyes, Livy. Did you get any sleep?"

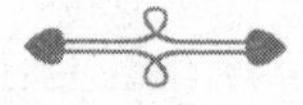

The plastic sheet that covered the empty window in the Temple had come loose at the top corner and was flapping like a bird's wing. Livy remembered how, on her first morning, she had looked up at the image of the boy stepping into the sky.

The teachers standing in front of them in the Temple all looked serious. Dr. Smythe, stone-faced, was staring at the pupils, as if she could look inside each and every one. Livy felt herself flush as the woman's eyes moved along Alex, Celia, and then stopped at Livy. She narrowed her eyes, looking at Livy with an increased attention. Livy looked down, flustered. Why was Dr. Smythe staring at her like that?

Mr. Bowen stood up and addressed the school.

"Last night, the school was broken into . . ."

Livy looked up, shocked. A murmur ran around the pupils.

"Dr. Smythe's study was ransacked. A number of extremely important pieces of research were removed and an enormous amount of damage was done."

Celia nudged her in the ribs. "I told you it was going to be something big. They'll have to get the police in."

Mr. Bowen continued, "At the moment, we are not sure who the thief could be, although we have some clues already."

Dr. Smythe tapped Mr. Bowen on the arm and leaned forward to say something.

Mr. Bowen nodded in agreement and again addressed the pupils. "If you see anything that you think might help us in our investigations, I would urge you to come and speak to me or Dr. Smythe."

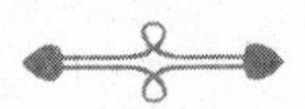

As they filed out of the Temple, Livy saw the two gray heads of Miss Jenkins and Miss Graves bent toward each other. "Her papers were thrown all over the floor." The woman's face was flushed with excitement—here was gossip indeed.

"And no sign of a forced entry!" Miss Graves hissed,

eyeing Livy and turning away. But Livy's hearing was sharper these days. "Even though the door remained locked."

"Perhaps the thief came down the chimney!"

"Or climbed in the window." The woman shivered. "But how could that be possible? It's too high!"

"You OK, Livy?" Celia nudged her. "You look funny."

"The boy," she whispered.

"What?" Celia looked surprised and looked around. "Have you seen Joe?"

Livy shook her head, and laughed over her embarrassment.

There was only one person who was as confident as she was on the roof. Only one person who could have climbed down and got into Dr. Smythe's study through the window.

What was he looking for?

CHAPTER TWENTY-TWO

As they walked back into the courtyard, Livy looked up at the Sentinel. Why would the boy break into Dr. Smythe's study? It made no sense. But, more worrying for her racing thoughts, she could see that there was no way that he could have gotten on to that windowsill.

Alex was thoughtful and subdued. "Someone must want to know what Dr. Smythe is up to. With her fascination with Master Burgess and his work . . . Oh, this is getting deeper and deeper . . ."

Celia stared at him. "I think you have some explaining to do, Alex. I have no idea what you are talking about."

"Think about the stained-glass window, Celia," Alex started off. "Did you ever think it was a strange image to have in a school? And dangerous, too. It could give someone really bad ideas about what to do on the top of a building."

As Alex spoke, a startling image dropped into Livy's mind: a row of boys standing on the roof.

"And then there's that phrase," Alex continued, "*tempus fugit.*"

"It's Latin, Alex." Celia rolled her eyes.

"Then there's the missing boy. Where did he go? What happened to him?" Alex's words were tumbling over and over one another.

But Celia wasn't listening. Joe Molyns had just walked by.

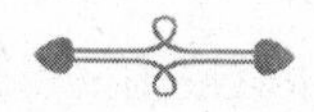

If Livy could have climbed up onto the roof and questioned the boy, she would have done so. But she had to wait until the evening. At home, Tom wanted "only Livy" to read him his bedtime story and then wanted another and another. He wanted to talk endlessly about Count Zacha, until Livy told him, quite sharply, that it was time to sleep.

As Livy jumped down onto the roof of the White Tower, she saw the boy, hardly more substantial than a shadow, sitting on his haunches, wrapped in the ragged black coat. His black hair fell across his brooding face.

He didn't move, didn't seem aware that anyone had joined him in his solitary musing. He looked entirely alone as he knotted his thin white fingers together.

"Hey!" she called out.

The boy turned his head, startled. Livy saw the gold flecks in his green eyes.

"I've been waiting for you," he said quietly. "For the longest time."

"Was it you?" Livy stepped toward him.

The boy looked puzzled. "What do you mean?"

"Dr. Smythe's study was broken into last night. Everything was destroyed. You shouldn't have done that."

"It wasn't me!" The boy's eyes flashed. "Although I would destroy all of Temple College if I could. I'd smash it to the ground and send it up in flames! I would do anything to stop what is about to happen." He took a step toward her. "You should stop what you are doing. You are playing with things you don't understand and can't control."

"But I'm helping you!" Livy cried. "I'm doing *your* experiment. In your room. I read your books. I'm sorry I ate your food, but I'm going to help you find a cure for . . ." Even as she said it she knew it sounded foolish. How could a powder made from gray metallic dust alter anything? "I am going to make a powder of alteration that will heal any sickness in the blood!"

The boy looked shocked and took a step back as if he had been pushed. He shook his head, trying to shake her words out of his mind.

He closed his eyes and took a deep breath. When he opened his eyes again, he looked calm. "You really want this. You want to change. To alter. To be something else. Well, I know a cure for the chaos in your blood. And it will work, believe me."

The boy tilted his face to the sky, flared his nostrils, and breathed in deeply so that his chest rose. He seemed to coil upward into the air. And, without Livy knowing how, or even seeing how, he was on the parapet of the roof. The wind took his black coat and it flapped like an enormous black wing. Something in the way he stood, looking down, right on the tips of his toes, frightened her.

"I don't want to be alone . . ." It was a small voice, a young child's voice. "Hold my hand."

It was what Mahalia had said to her the last time Livy had seen her. But it wasn't Mahalia on the roof. Another child stood next to the boy. And a man wearing a long dark cloak. The man raised his arms, and, as if this were a signal, Livy saw the boy bend his knees.

"Be careful!" Livy cried out, but the wind took her words, blew away the image of the child and the cloaked man. The boy leaned even further into the empty air. "Stop!" Livy lunged forward to grab him back.

"I've seen the smoke at the window . . ." The boy's words swirled around her. He was on the brink of falling, she was sure. So why didn't he? How could he hang in the air like that?

"Please . . ." Livy tried to control her voice. She sensed that if she startled him, he would fall. She put out her arm to pull him back and just as her fingers grazed the inky black of his coat, he turned toward her. His eyes sparkled, the gold glinting in the green.

"Why don't you come closer, Livy," he whispered. He leaned even farther forward.

"You're going to fall," Livy blurted out. Her nerves were screwed tight. She no longer felt mixed with the air and the night. Her legs felt heavy and she could hardly breathe. She grabbed the sleeve of his coat, but he shook her off.

"Come up here," he said. "Come and stand next to me."

In spite of herself, she put out her hand and pulled herself onto the parapet.

"Don't be frightened." The boy's voice was soft and reassuring. "It seems hard at first, but you learn to trust yourself and do it."

"Do what?" Livy looked at the angle of the boy's body. She felt her own body tilt.

"You know what," he said. And she *did* know.

Livy looked down at the flagstones. She felt the blood leap in her veins.

"You won't know if you don't try," the boy whispered

as the wind moved his hair across his moon-white face. "Imagine . . . to mix your blood with the air and sweep through the heavens, the stars at your heels . . ." His lip trembled. "Leave all the heaviness and unhappiness down there and come with me. Don't you want to? I can take you wherever you want to go."

Livy's toes were right on the edge of the roof. She could imagine herself turning and swooping through the infinite sky in a body that was weightless. Or perhaps she was feeling the sky moving through her skin and bones that were no more substantial than smoke.

"We can fly through star nurseries"—the boy's whispered voice urged her and his words threw up images of great chambers of colored clouds with pinpoints of bright light—"as we chase comets' tails toward ancient suns."

Livy felt the last of the weight of her body balanced on the very tip of her toes, her muscles twitched as if she would jump.

"Do it," the boy whispered. "You can't know what will happen until you . . ."

But the scream of a siren and the flashing lights of an ambulance tearing up the embankment knocked Livy out of the moment.

"Will it hurt?" she gasped, pulling herself back. "If I fall?"

"You won't fall"—the boy's voice was rich and full of the starlight he promised her—"if you hold my hand." He put out his white hand to her. All she had to do was grasp those fingers and step into the sky. She reached out her hand, but her fingers didn't quite meet his. "Trust me," he whispered.

Livy put her foot out into the air.

"Up there," the boy's voice drifted toward her, "the clouds are made of emeralds and sapphires and the sky is an endless rainbow."

Livy felt her heels rise up off the parapet.

"That's right," he said, his voice reassuring. "It's just a step away."

Livy looked up into the infinite sky. She leaned toward him and stretched out her fingers.

"Close your eyes." The boy's voice was hardly more than breath. "We will mix our blood with the air."

She would fall—they both would. But perhaps that was what she wanted. To fall. Just a moment in the air, not much of a price to pay to see Mahalia again . . .

She tipped forward, felt the air press against her . . .

Her stomach turned. What was she doing?

"Wait!" she cried. "I'm frightened!" Livy felt a little tug on her hand. The air around her quivered.

She opened her eyes. She was alone. Of course he'd been playing with her, had enjoyed making a fool of her, was probably even now laughing at her from behind one of the chimney pots.

"I didn't believe you!" she yelled. "Not for one second!" She felt small and foolish. "And you can keep your stupid roof!"

CHAPTER TWENTY-THREE

Shocked at what the boy had almost made her do, Livy climbed down to the room at the top of the White Tower. If she saw him in the room, she would tell him exactly what she thought of him. But she wasn't concentrating, her thoughts taken up with how she had felt on the edge of the roof, how she had nearly stepped into the air. She missed putting her foot onto the metal bracket that attached the drainpipe to the wall. She nearly fell and clung to the cold metal, frightened and tearful. How could she have been so stupid? She had put her trust in someone and look what had happened—she had nearly thrown herself into the air. He had told her that this would be a cure for the chaos in her blood. And now she was clinging to the side of the White Tower, too scared to move.

She had to force herself to jump onto the window ledge, her eyes closed, expecting to fall, and cried out with relief as she pushed open the shutter.

The fire was burning, there was food on the table, and a book left open on the desk in the place where the other book, the book she had thrown on the fire, was usually left. "How dare he make fun of me like that," she muttered.

Livy lifted the heavy flask of gray dust. Her pulse was so violent that her hands shook.

Her anger subsided as images flickered in her mind. The boy had hung in the air. She saw the angle of his body again in her mind's eye. The gray powder inside the flask jumped.

"Help him."

Livy swung around. "Who's there?" she called out. But she knew that singsong voice, she knew who had spoken to her. "Mahalia?"

"He's so lonely."

Livy closed her eyes to hang on to the clearness of Mahalia's voice. Would the girl speak to her again? She cried out as her hand jerked up as if someone had pushed it, hard.

Livy opened her eyes to see the dust swirling in the bottom of the glass. She watched in surprise as three large droplets of red liquid appeared on the side of the glass and trickled down to be swallowed greedily. Livy looked at her hand; she had cut it on a chip in the neck of the flask when her arm had been jerked upward.

She lifted her fingers to her mouth, tasting the salt and iron in her blood.

In the depths of the tower a door slammed shut. And now she could hear footsteps running up the stone stairs. The boy? Well, she wouldn't let him laugh at her! It wouldn't be long until the door in the corner of the room burst open. She had to leave, and quickly. She lunged at the window and climbed out.

She had left the shutters open enough that she could see just the bench. For a few minutes, she could hear someone moving around in the room, but she couldn't see who it was.

And then she saw a figure, but it was not the boy. A woman, dressed in blue velvet, a sheet of blond hair falling across her face as she leaned over Livy's flask. Even though she knew that her experiment was worthless, even though she had enjoyed watching that book go up in flames, seeing Dr. Smythe so engrossed in the contents of the flask made Livy angry.

"Keep away from my things," Livy whispered through her clenched jaw. "Don't touch anything!"

But even as she said those words, Dr. Smythe bent forward and lifted the flask.

"How interesting," the woman mused.

"Put it down," Livy wanted to cry out to her. "It isn't interesting to you! Your work is on gravity. Why do you care what's in my flask? That won't help you."

Because, Livy now realized, her work with the metal and the candle was harmless, a waste of time.

Dr. Smythe picked up the flask and shook it. Livy saw her smile by the light of the fire as the contents jumped.

"This is just what I was hoping for." The woman tapped the glass with her nail. "The experiment that will finish Alan Hopkins for good. *Tempus fugit?* Hah! Time will not fly for him. He'll be done for. I have everything in this one little flask to ruin him."

Livy felt light-headed. She swayed on the window ledge and had to grab at the window to prevent herself falling. The noise startled Dr. Smythe, who looked up, frowning. Livy pressed herself into the stone as the woman quickly crossed the room and slammed the shutter closed.

That dear little room, Livy's refuge, had been ruined by the presence of that woman. The work that Livy had done, trying to make a powder of alteration, would now somehow be used to harm poor Mr. Hopkins.

"Help him . . . He's so lonely."

Mahalia's voice.

Moments later, Livy had grabbed at the drainpipe and scrabbled for the roof, almost falling as she put her hand out to heave herself onto the parapet.

She had only managed to pull one leg onto the roof.

"You've done it now!" the boy's voice spat at her.

Livy stood up.

"I've done nothing," she exclaimed.

"Who will save him?" The boy's arm shot out and he gave her a little push. "When the time comes!"

She toppled slightly. "Hey! Stop that!"

The boy scowled, unrepentant.

Livy took to the roof, tears pricking at her eyes.

CHAPTER TWENTY-FOUR

"I'm going to big school." Tom sat on the end of Livy's bed. Livy felt as if she had fallen asleep only moments before, but it was already morning. "I've got big school boots on."

"Clear off," she said, lifting her legs and tipping Tom slowly toward the floor. He squealed in delight. "This big girl has got to get her uniform on."

By the time she got downstairs, her father was already in his heavy winter coat, a scarf wrapped around his neck.

"Do you have to go so early?" Livy's mother asked him, still wearing her dressing gown.

"Lots to do," her father muttered. "I wish I'd never signed up for this 'take a child to work' day. It was Dr. Smythe's idea. You'd think she sees enough children at Temple College, but she seemed *very* keen to have Tom."

"Well, he is adorable, James."

"You keep him today, then!"

"You can't disappoint him," Livy's mother said. "He's been looking forward to it. And so have I! I'm going out all day!"

Tom jumped up and down in his "big school boots." "Can we go? Can we go?"

"Hang on, tiger." Livy's father sighed, wearily. "Have you said good-bye to your mother? Otherwise she'll cry and cry and cry all day long."

"Good-bye," Tom said seriously. "Don't be sad while I'm gone."

"And a kiss for Livy?"

Tom blew Livy a raspberry.

"Do you have your briefcase? You can't go to the office without it!"

Tom lifted up his Count Zacha lunch box. "Let's fly!"

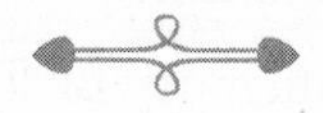

The air was so cold as Livy stepped out of the house some minutes later that it caught at her throat. She pulled her scarf up over her mouth and pushed her hands deep in her pockets.

She was relieved to see Mr. Hopkins waiting at the end of Leaden Lane. "You mustn't stay here," she said, slightly out of breath from running toward him. "You have to leave and leave now. If Dr. Smythe sees you . . ." She shivered,

not because of the cold but because she again heard that biting tone of pleasure in the woman's voice: *He'll be done for.*

Mr. Hopkins looked anxious. "But my books, Miss Burgess. I find it so hard to leave them." He coughed.

"Dr. Smythe is serious," Livy said.

The man sighed. "So it's good-bye."

Livy nodded.

"I feel I should thank you, Miss Burgess."

"I've not done very much for you. In fact, it's my family's fault that you have no home and no job."

"Oh, you mustn't be too hard on the Burgesses." Mr. Hopkins smiled sadly. "You have done more for me than you can ever know. I saw your little brother walk past a few minutes ago." He chuckled to himself. "I wonder if he's perfected his landings yet."

Livy smiled at the memory of Tom showing off.

"He's a character." Mr. Hopkins looked at his watch. "Ah, well, time for me to go." He coughed again. "Places to go. People to meet."

Livy thought she had never seen someone less likely to have anywhere to go. The man looked as if he was trying to be brave as he raised his hat to bid a final farewell. "*Tempus fugit,* Miss Burgess."

Livy waited on the corner of Leaden Lane and watched as he walked away.

"Poor man," she said to herself as she went into school. "Poor, lonely man sent away by Dr. Smythe."

But Livy felt uncomfortable, too. She had something to do with this—her father had taken the man's job and she had made something in the White Tower that Dr. Smythe would have used against Mr. Hopkins had he stayed. But how could the contents of Livy's flask—just a teaspoon of metal filings—be of any use to Dr. Smythe?

When the headmistress passed Livy in the corridor, Livy felt her cheeks flare up with anger at the woman's heartlessness toward such a feeble old man.

"I just saw your brother," Alex said to Livy as they lined up to go into the dining hall.

"My dad brought him to work today," Livy muttered, her thoughts still on Dr. Smythe and the room in the tower.

"I didn't see him in the library"—Alex frowned—"or with your dad. He was coming out of Dr. Smythe's study."

Alex was right. As Livy entered the dining hall, she saw Tom sitting at the top table, next to Dr. Smythe, eating a plate of fries, his face very serious.

"She can't have Tom," Livy said to Alex.

"But he's having a lovely time," Alex frowned. "What are you worried about?"

Tom saw Livy at that moment and he waved excitedly. He shook Dr. Smythe's arm and pointed at Livy. Dr. Smythe smiled down at him, saying something that Livy couldn't hear.

"I'm going to tell her to leave him alone." Livy thrust her tray at Alex.

"What are you doing?" Celia grabbed her arm and pulled her back down onto the bench. "You don't just march up to Dr. Smythe and tell her what to do!"

"But she's got my brother!"

"And he's having a lovely time." Celia waved at Tom who waved back. "What's got into you today, Livy? You're so on edge."

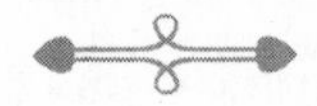

At the start of afternoon classes, Alex said he was going to the library. "If anyone asks, just say I've gone to the nurse's office. Tell them I've got a headache."

"Keep an eye out for Tom," Livy said as Alex walked away. Alex gave her a thumbs-up.

Their usual French teacher, Madame Smith, was ill, and her place was taken by another member of staff who didn't notice that Alex was absent.

Perhaps it was the change of teacher, but Livy found it hard to concentrate. The air in the brightly lit classroom seemed heavy and thick. She was happy when they changed classrooms and walked up to the physics lab, which looked out over the Court of Sentinels.

"And where is Alex?" Mr. Bowen asked as they took their places.

"He's in the nurse's office," Celia said. Livy heard Martha snigger behind them. "He's got a headache."

"A headache?" Mr. Bowen peered at her over his glasses.

"It's the lights, sir," Celia offered. "They affect his vision and then he gets migraines."

"Migraines?" Mr. Bowen took off his glasses. "Perhaps you'd let him know, Celia, that if I find that he has spent the afternoon in the library, he will be in trouble." He put his glasses back on.

Livy looked out the window. Dusk was already falling around the Sentinel on the roof of the White Tower. She realized that she would not be going back now that Dr. Smythe had discovered her laboratory. She would never again tuck herself under the Sentinel's broken wing and look up at Mahalia's star.

"Sorry I didn't say good-bye," Livy whispered to the sad stone face.

"Let's get this physics done!" Mr. Bowen said to the class. "Unless anyone else has an allergic reaction to lightbulbs!"

Livy's phone buzzed in her pocket. She pulled it out discreetly. Mr. Bowen often ended the lesson with a pile of phones on his desk that had been confiscated. She glanced at the screen. Alex! So annoying. *I'm in the archive room! I'm going back in time.*

"Put your phone away," Celia said, aware of what Livy was doing even though her eyes were fixed on the board. "Mr. Bowen's looking."

Livy quickly typed, *Did you see Tom?*

I heard him. I had to hide. But don't you want to know what I found?

Livy only wanted to know about Tom.

Another message. *I was right! There were seven scholars, not six as it says on the board.*

Can you go and check on Tom?

In a minute. Don't you want to know who the lost boy is?

Not really!

He was called Ralph Symons. Fifteen years old. And he didn't die. He was sent to another place.

Livy put her phone away. There were only moments until the end of school; she was eager for the day to be over and to get home and be with Tom.

She looked out the window.

A lost boy sent to another place.

Livy squinted as the dusk gathered over the Sentinel. She was being foolish. Alex's words had gotten to her and her imagination was playing tricks because Tom was safe now, surely. Safe in the library with her father.

But Tom, her Tom with his messy curls and rounded forehead, was leaning over the parapet of the White Tower. He seemed to be looking for something in the clouds. Livy stood up and her sudden movement must have caught his eye because he turned to look toward the classroom.

And now she saw another figure. Dr. Smythe was also standing on the roof just a few feet away. She was waving her arms, encouraging Tom to do something, but do what?

"What are you doing?" she heard Celia say, but Livy couldn't speak. She was fixated on Tom's little face as he smiled excitedly, and waved at her.

"Sit down!" Mr. Bowen told her, but Livy didn't move.

"Tom," Livy whispered. "On the tower."

Tom now turned his head as if he was listening to something. Dr. Smythe! He stepped back, lost to her view.

"There's no one there, Livy." Celia was pulling at Livy's blazer sleeve. "Everyone's looking."

"Martha!" Livy heard Mr. Bowen snap. "Hand your phone over."

"But, sir!"

"I can see you taking pictures! Hand it over. And don't think you're getting it back until tomorrow."

"But, *sir!*"

The lesson bell rang. Chairs scraped and voices rose.

"Livy?" Mr. Bowen said her name. "Can I have a word?"

Livy couldn't move. Her stomach was in knots. She felt as if she couldn't breathe.

"What's the matter?" Celia pulled at her arm, but Livy shook her off.

"Headache," she gasped. "Sorry, sir. I have to go home and lie down." And she stumbled from the classroom.

CHAPTER TWENTY-FIVE

Livy threw open her bedroom window, heaved herself out, and scrambled up toward the roof. "Please don't let it be Tom," she said to herself as she ran. She had been playing too many games, pretending to herself that she could hear Mahalia, speaking to her from her hiding place behind a star, seeing shadowy children on the roof, so perhaps that image of Tom up there, waving to her so happily, was just another image that her mind, going too far this time, had conjured up.

"Please don't let it be Tom," she said again, her breath coming in ragged gasps. She threw herself at the air, careless, desperate. "Please don't let Dr. Smythe do anything bad to him."

"Livy! Oh, thank goodness. Quick . . . it's Tom!" Dr. Smythe was not standing on the roof of the White Tower, she was a few feet away on the roof above her study.

"Stay away from him!" Livy leapt to block the woman who tried to take a step forward. She wobbled. Livy saw that she had no shoes on.

"Livy!" Tom jumped up and down.

"Stay where you are, Tom." Livy gasped in surprise as Mr. Hopkins stepped from behind the Sentinel's wing. "Livy has come to help us. Dr. Smythe won't take you now, Tom. Livy won't allow it."

"But . . . but . . . you've gone!" Livy said to the man.

"Oh, but I had to save the boy from Dr. Smythe, Livy," Mr. Hopkins said. "She wants him for a terrible experiment! Your father was no help, virtually handed the boy to her on a plate! Oh, I only just got here in time!"

"Livy!" Dr. Smythe cried. Livy spun around to see the woman, who had tears in her eyes. "Don't listen to him."

"She might seem very convincing," Mr. Hopkins said. "But inside that woman beats an evil heart, Livy."

Dr. Smythe seemed to be having trouble on the roof. Casting her eyes to the ground, she swayed. "Oh no, Livy," she whispered. "I feel as if the ground is going to swallow me." She sank to her knees.

"She wants Tom, Livy," Mr. Hopkins hissed. "Quick! Push her! Or she'll have him!"

Livy took a step toward Dr. Smythe, who looked as if something was pressing her down. Her eyes were closed. She put her hands to the lead, clinging on as if she were on a life raft and the waves were about to drown her.

"Forgive me," she whispered. "I did everything I could . . ." The woman slumped forward. "I can't move. If I move, I will fall, I'm sure of it . . . Ah . . . *Vertigo*."

"Such a drama queen." Mr. Hopkins tutted. He had taken Tom by the hand.

"Now, Tom." Livy heard Mr. Hopkins's voice, no longer frail and trembling but clear and confident. "Are you ready? Are you looking into the sky? Can you see Count Zacha?"

Livy couldn't understand why Mr. Hopkins was holding Tom so tightly by the hand that his bony knuckles were white.

"Livy!" Tom cried out joyfully. "Have you come to see Count Zacha, too?" He tugged on Mr. Hopkins's hand hard, as if he would run toward her, but he was held tight. Tom looked up in surprise at the thin old man who held him so firmly.

"Don't spoil things for the boy," Mr. Hopkins hissed at Livy. "He's very excited. It's bad enough that you've turned up. I really hoped that you wouldn't come. It's so annoying when things don't go entirely to plan."

"Can Livy come, too?" Tom looked up hopefully at Mr. Hopkins.

"I'm sorry, Tom, I don't think that she can," Mr. Hopkins said as he pulled his thin face into an exaggeratedly sad expression, like a clown. "Count Zacha doesn't have room for two people in that very small Warrior Copter of his. Also, she's not as brave as you. She's a girl."

"Let go of him!" Livy tried to lunge at Tom, but Mr. Hopkins merely pulled him out of her reach.

"I don't need wings to fly, Livy," Tom said proudly. "I am brave and my blood is as light as air!"

"Indeed. All the heaviness will soon be altered." Mr. Hopkins looked at Livy, his eyes glittering. "Livy knows all about that, Tom. She has spent many nights trying to alter her own blood."

He spoke so calmly and Tom was so happy that Livy thought perhaps she was mistaken thinking that Tom could come to any harm. Perhaps they were just playing a game about Count Zacha.

But it was a strange sort of game.

"Now, hold out your hands and close your eyes."

Tom snapped his eyes shut and held out his hands.

"And you shall have a big surprise."

Mr. Hopkins pulled a glass flask out of his coat pocket. It was Livy's flask from the White Tower, the flask with the chipped top. The rim had a dark crust of her blood. And inside was her stupid, useless powder of alteration—

the powder that altered nothing! Mr. Hopkins sprinkled the gray dust into Tom's upturned palms. The wind caught the grainy powder—Livy smelled that intoxicating, familiar scent of burning metal—and blew it away from Tom. A gray flake landed on Livy's hand; it stung like an insect bite.

"Now. Rub it in your hair, Tom," Mr. Hopkins said, oblivious to the fact that there was barely any powder on Tom's hands. "Just like I told you, and then we will be ready for Count Zacha!"

Tom rubbed his hands through his hair.

"Please, Mr. Hopkins." Livy took a step toward Tom. "Let him go. He's only little. I don't know what sort of game you are playing with him, but he's too young to understand."

Mr. Hopkins stared at Livy in surprise. "You don't want Tom to meet Count Zacha?" he asked, blinking. "After he's spent every night for weeks staring out of his window waiting for him to arrive? Well, why didn't you say that you wanted to disappoint him?" The man bent down and stared into Tom's serious face. Some of the powder in Tom's hair had fallen on to his face and must have gotten into his eyes, because he started to blink back tears.

"Livy thinks you don't want to meet your friend," Mr. Hopkins said seriously. "She thinks you would rather go home with her."

Tom sniffed, looking into Mr. Hopkins's drawn, hollow face. He seemed mesmerized by the man's voice.

"Would you like that?"

Tom shook his head slowly.

Mr. Hopkins stood up. "He doesn't want to come with you, I'm afraid."

"Tom?" Livy whispered. "Come to me." She took another step toward Tom but he moved behind Mr. Hopkins and watched her mournfully.

"I want to see Count Zacha," Tom said. "I have been good—as good as gold—so he will come."

"We don't have much time, Livy." Mr. Hopkins narrowed his eyes. "*Tempus fugit* and all that. Although I can't resist thanking you for helping me."

"Helping you?" Livy felt as if she was on the edge of something, about to fall. "How could I have helped you?"

"By working so hard to make a powder of alteration!"

Livy felt as if someone had hit her on the side of her head. She swayed slightly.

"You think I didn't know? But who do you think found out that you were related to Peter Burgess, the first headmaster of Temple College, if not me rummaging around in the school archives? And who do you think arranged for your father's swift appointment to the job I had held for forty years if not me? Dr. Smythe would never have found you!"

"Livy—be careful . . . Oh! Why can't I move? This fear of falling . . . I daren't . . . I can't . . . My head is spinning . . . I will fall . . ." Dr. Smythe's voice, husky with fear, cut across Mr. Hopkins.

"You still there?" the man cried out. "Calm down, dear! Move along! Nothing to see here!" He sighed. "Women! Always meddling!" He pulled a wry face. "Now. Where was I? Yes, of course, with Master Burgess, a true genius, whose work I have been in awe of and studied all the many years I have spent in the library of Temple College. But do you know? I'm sure this will surprise you, but however hard I tried, I could not match his talents! I failed to make a powder of alteration. But you . . . *you* . . . with the Burgess blood in your veins, succeeded where I had failed."

"But I didn't make anything!" Livy cried out, appalled at what she was hearing. "It was just some metal filings in a flask!"

"Oh, you're far too humble," Mr. Hopkins chuckled. "Metal filings, yes, but they were carefully purified through an alchemical process. And your blood, Livy. Don't forget your precious Burgess blood. Oh, I knew you'd do it, even though you lost those pages I slipped into the book about the seagull. You threw them off the tower, do you remember? Tut-tut." He wagged a finger at her. "But no matter. I was able to find other books by Peter Burgess that helped you in your work. I have been watching you, Livy, so carefully since the day that you arrived, encouraging you."

Livy remembered then . . . that feeling she was being watched, that dark figure scuttling down the street.

"In fact, I watched you more closely than your foolish, negligent mother and father! But then, that's modern parents for you, always worried about how much time their children are spending on their phones and never thinking that their daughter is climbing out onto the roof every night! Did you like the cookies I left for you? The cordial? The books?"

"That was you? I thought the room was Dr. Smythe's!"

"She did get in. Poked her bony nose around. But, being a stupid *scientist,* she had no idea what she was looking at! There she was in the room in the White Tower that I have used as my private laboratory for years! With every important book on alchemy ever written! She thought no one could get in because she had the only key. But she didn't think about you and your ability to climb over roofs. Or me and my underground passage from the library. People can be so blind and scientists are the worst! Do you know that I've been sleeping in the library ever since I was fired? I made a little bed out of my books. Remarkably comfortable. Your father's cookies sustained me. And no one sees what is happening! But then, that fool of a father of yours is just as blind. He's in his little cubicle now, while you and

Tom are on the roof, looking for all the books I've hidden."

The man laughed a thin little laugh, more like a cough, and put his arm protectively around Tom. He bared his gray teeth in a semblance of a smile.

"Almost time, Tom. Would you be so kind as to climb up now? I think I can hear Count Zacha approaching."

Instead of climbing up on his own, Tom lifted up his arms and Mr. Hopkins, surprisingly strong for someone so small and thin, swung him up and placed him lightly on the parapet.

"Stop!" Livy cried out. "Please!"

"Oh, he'll come to no harm," Mr. Hopkins sniggered. "You saw the picture in the window in the Temple before it was destroyed—a boy who could step into the sky. Master Burgess put that picture in the window as a tribute to his great final experiment. A triumphant gesture of a man who had finally found the secret of how to make a boy's blood so light that it would float into the air and the boy would fly like an angel!"

He gave Tom a little push. The boy wobbled, but, his face startled, he managed to correct himself. Mr. Hopkins hardly noticed.

"No need for farewells, adieus, or à bientôts. Fly, little Tom. Quick quick! Chop chop. Tally ho!" he cried. "Show Livy what you can do now that her powder of alteration has transformed you into an angel!"

Livy threw herself forward. Why was Mr. Hopkins laughing?

"Tom!" she cried. "Don't listen to him! Just come to me, please!"

Tom turned his head. "Livy. I can fly!" But she saw that he was shocked by her expression. Fear flickered across his soft features. "Livy?" he whispered.

"Taking too long!" Mr. Hopkins's arm shot out. It was just a gentle push, no more than a tap on his shoulder, but Tom lost his balance. Livy heard his soft gasp of surprise as she scrambled up onto the parapet.

Livy jumped.

CHAPTER TWENTY-SIX

She had him by the hand!

She clutched Tom's fingers tight. He wasn't heavy.

They should be falling, both of them, toward the ground. But they hung in the air. It was very quiet, no sound of the traffic below. No sound, even, of the wind in the trees below. The air around them was soft, like a pillow, and she felt her body settle as if she had stepped onto a solid and invisible cloud. Time, like Livy, was suspended.

She looked around. She was just below the roofline. If she put her hand out, the hand that was not holding on to Tom's wrist so tightly, she could easily pull herself back up. She tilted her head and looked at the infinite sky, at the clouds, which seemed larger and more beautiful than ever before. Her hair spread out around her as if she were in the swimming pool. She breathed in and she could no longer tell where she stopped and the air began. She felt as if she were made from marshmallows and cherry blossoms. So this was the feeling that she had been trying to resist for so long.

"Livy," Tom whispered. "I can't see Count Zacha. If he doesn't come and carry me away soon, I will fall." A fat tear rolled down his flushed cheek.

And then Livy realized that she was still in the air. She looked at the ground and saw her feet hanging there. They must fall soon . . . She flinched as she imagined hitting the ground, felt the fear rush in . . .

She tried to push Tom back onto the roof. But she was stuck. The air around them would not budge. And she began to feel the weight of Tom's body, which up to then had been no heavier than a balloon. But now he was getting heavier and heavier and dragging her down, his little fingers slipping through her own. It was as if whatever mechanism controlled time and gravity was beginning to work, albeit not very smoothly, once more.

She forced herself to pull him up toward her. Her arms ached and she thought they would come out of their sockets. Tom squirmed.

"Stay still," she cried. "If you move, I can't help you."

Slowly, agonizingly, she lifted Tom up onto the parapet just above her, and held on as he climbed back down onto the roof. She'd done it—he was safe. It was too much to think that she had saved Tom but that she might not be able to save herself.

She looked back up to see Mr. Hopkins standing above her. He wasn't looking at Tom anymore.

"Extraordinary," he breathed. "The boy did not fall. And even held up the girl! The powder must be powerful indeed."

"Please," Livy heard herself whimper. She was no longer full of air. That had all been squeezed out of her by a fear, a force darker and heavier than gravity. Her legs were heavy and getting heavier, pulling her down. Her hands were slipping as she tried to grip onto the dry stone of the parapet.

Mr. Hopkins said nothing but took off his hat and threw it away from him. Then he threw another handful of gray powder over his bald head. He smiled. "So Tom has proved that it works!" he cried. "The powder of alteration works!" He seemed to become younger—the creases in his skin were now smooth and his face shone as if it had been polished. His eyes sparkled. His voice rang out like a bell.

"I feel how I am being transformed," he cried. "I feel the Burgess powder refining me. The dross will be burned away and my base flesh will become a new sort of gold. I can feel my blood growing brighter, filling with air. It is the transformation we all seek!"

Mr. Hopkins raised his foot shod in that shabby cracked brogue and placed it on Livy's hand. The pain was unbearable. Livy felt the bones crack as he pressed down.

"The sky is mine"—the man held up his arms—"and all of time, too." He licked his lips. "You should have paid closer attention to the work of the alchemists of Temple College, Livy," he whispered. "Their work was secret, conducted in locked laboratories, but they left so many clues around the school. *Tempus fugit.* Time flies! Those words! They're written all over the school and yet no one stopped to think what they really mean! If you had been brave enough to understand those words, you might have been standing where I am, now, the whole of time and space at your command! The whole of time to fly through!" He shook his head as if he felt genuinely sorry for her. "You, Miss Burgess, with the blood of a master alchemist running through your veins, will never be transformed!"

"Please," Livy croaked. "Help me."

Mr. Hopkins seemed oblivious to Livy; he was speaking as if he was giving a speech that he had memorized. "There was a moment when I saw you stand right on the edge of the roof and I thought you might be brave enough, but you stepped back. You didn't believe what Peter Burgess knew."

"Please, Mr. Hopkins . . . I can't hold on much longer."

"What did Peter Burgess discover?" The man put his head to one side. "He was the first man to realize that when an object falls, it is subject to gravity. Years before

Isaac Newton!" He laughed. "But you know that, don't you? You can feel the effects of it dragging your body to the ground right now. And once your arms get too tired to hang on any longer, you will fall to the flagstones. But what you won't realize, you silly timid girl, is that not only are you falling through space, you are falling through time! It will be perhaps half a second after your hand leaves this parapet that your body hits the floor. You will have moved through time. That is what Peter Burgess understood. Gravity and time are interlocked." Mr. Hopkins twisted two shining fingers together. "So just think. If you gain mastery over one"—Mr. Hopkins took a deep breath, closing his eyes—"you have the other in your grasp."

Livy tried to swing her legs up onto the parapet, but Mr. Hopkins's eyes snapped open. He wagged a finger at her. "Naughty, naughty, Livy. You will fall when I am ready. I want you to see what you could have had. What you could have been!" He took his foot off Livy's hand and bent down until his face was close to Livy's. His breath smelled of smoke. "Imagine"—Mr. Hopkins's face blazed—"having the power to alter your *human blood to angelic . . . and fly . . .*"

"Please, Mr. Hopkins," Livy pleaded. "Just let me back on to the roof. Tom will be frightened." She couldn't see Tom, but she could hear him whispering to himself.

"Master Burgess was not interested in the wealth and riches of this world!" Mr. Hopkins cried. "It was just a simple change, Livy, not painful at all. And the boy that Master Burgess picked for his secret experiment should have been grateful. The powder made him perfect, made him immortal, and it must have been beautiful when he stepped into the sky!" He laughed. "To be perfect, to live forever, that's what Master Burgess discovered. Do you see my skin?" Mr. Hopkins pulled up the sleeve on his frayed shirt sleeve. Livy squinted as the man's skin flashed in the sunlight. "The powder is altering my blood; it is making me immortal. Today, I will walk with the angels!"

Mr. Hopkins jumped up onto the parapet. "And so, I step into the air," he declared to the sky. "Gravity, that mortal force, cannot claim me." His lips, no longer gray and thin, but red and full, quivered with excitement. He looked down at Livy, his eyes flashing. "Watch as the air embraces me. The infinite sky awaits!"

And Livy saw the brown brogue shoe hang in the air beside her.

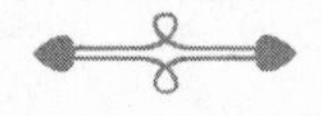

There was a draft of air, a gasp of surprise, and, in less than a heartbeat, a dull thud. That was all. No cry, no

sound of any distress. The space where the man had stood was empty.

Livy could see the ground out of the corner of her eye. But there was no body, just something that looked like a pile of gray ash where Mr. Hopkins had fallen.

"Livy?" It was Dr. Smythe. "Has he gone? I can't see! I can't lift my head. I daren't move or I'll fall. Is Tom safe?"

Livy tried once more to pull herself up, but it was hopeless. Her arms had no strength left in them.

In one more heartbeat, she would fall.

There was a blue star hanging in the violet sky above the Sentinel. That would be the last thing she saw: Mahalia's star. She closed her eyes. Her fingers slipped on the stone.

But then, she felt cool fingers on her hands! They stroked her fingers and her bones no longer hurt. Her heart leapt with relief. She opened her eyes.

"It's you!" she cried out to the boy with gold-flecked green eyes. "Help me!" But then, as her fingers slipped again and he did nothing to help her, she breathed, "You're not a dream, are you?"

The boy shook his head, slowly. "No, Livy," he whispered. He smiled, a long, languorous smile that had no sense of urgency in it. "I am not a dream."

Why was he still leaning over her, smiling that way? Why wasn't he hauling her up over the parapet?

"Then help me!" Livy spat the words out. Her arms were trembling with the effort of holding on. The clouds were heavy above her, the air was still silent. It was as if everything around her was hanging, just like her, in the second before the fall.

And still the boy did nothing. His hand was on hers, but he just stared down at her with his beautiful, mesmerizing eyes. The flecks began to dance in the deep emerald of his irises.

"Please," Livy begged. "I don't know your name."

"Ralph." She watched his smile deepen as he said his name. "Ralph Symons."

Livy heard a loud roar in her ears. "But . . . Alex just told me . . . Ralph Symons is the name of the lost boy . . . hundreds of years ago. He's dead by now."

"Do I look dead?" The boy frowned.

"Ralph . . . I can't hold on."

At this, the boy nodded and whispered, "Of course. You need help." He pushed one of his fingers under her clawed forefinger and slowly lifted it away from the stone.

Pain shot through her hand. "What are you doing?" She screamed, again trying to pull herself up. "Help me!"

He shook his head sadly. "You don't need any help, Livy," his voice scarcely more than breath. She saw tears spring up in his eyes.

"But I'm going to fall!" Livy glanced down. "Let go

of my hand!" she cried out to the boy, tears pricking her eyes. "Stop doing that! Why aren't you helping me?"

She could see Tom's face as he clung to the Sentinel's wing. His mouth was open, but no sound came out. He held out his hand to her, but didn't move.

Livy slipped below the parapet.

"I can't help you." The boy lifted another of her fingers and held it away from the stone. She cried out again, a strangled noise gargling at the back of her throat.

"No one can help you, Livy," Ralph said, his voice now so quiet that Livy wasn't sure that he was even speaking. Perhaps he was only moving his lips. "You can only help yourself."

Her hands came free.

She heard herself cry out.

She was falling backward, facing the sky, and the Sentinel whose gentle face looked sad.

"Good-bye, Tom," Livy breathed. She should have hit the ground by now, but the minute she was in was stretching out, expanding to fill the air around her. "I'm sorry that I can't stay with you. I'm sure someone will come for you soon. I hope they do. I don't want you to be frightened." She was aware that her thoughts weren't rushed or hurried and that she was still staring at the heavy sky. Perhaps she had already fallen? She shivered as the thought crossed her mind. Perhaps she was already dead.

She felt herself bounce, as if she had hit something.

"I told you not to be frightened," Ralph whispered. He hung in the air next to her.

"Why aren't you falling?" Livy gasped.

"Why aren't you?"

"I . . . I . . ."

"We have been altered, Livy. By Burgess blood."

CHAPTER TWENTY-SEVEN

He pulled her back up to the roof; everything was quiet. Tom didn't move. It was as if he were asleep, although his eyes were open. He had put his thumb in his mouth. Dr. Smythe lay on the roof just a few feet away. She must have tried so hard to reach Tom, Livy thought, before she had collapsed.

"How is this happening?" Livy and Ralph sat, shoulder to shoulder, on the parapet. The stars were the only thing that had any life to them; they twinkled in the dark winter sky.

"Master Burgess made me," the boy explained.

"But that can't be," Livy whispered. "Master Burgess died centuries ago."

"And he made me centuries ago. *Tempus fugit,*" Ralph whispered. "I was made to step into the air like an angel, outside the force that pulls all bodies to the ground, to never know again what it is to walk the earth. I was made to step over time."

"But how is such a thing possible?"

"Master Burgess believed that mortals could be perfect—like angels—if only he could lighten their blood." Ralph frowned. "He began to experiment."

"To find a powder of alteration?"

"There were other boys, too," Ralph said sadly. "Better scholars than me, more able with their numbers and keener at their studies. He chose us. He trained us. He brought us up here. I had never been up so high! I thought I could reach up and touch the clouds. But then another boy, one of the young ones, started crying."

"I saw you," Livy whispered. "On the roof. That boy was so small."

Livy saw again the row of seven boys standing on the roof of the White Tower. A man in a long dark robe stood behind them. He sprinkled some dust on each boy's head in turn. And then the boys climbed up onto the parapet. Livy couldn't hear what was being said, but one boy, much younger than the others, with hair like Tom's, was looking up at Ralph. He tugged on Ralph's sleeve, but Livy could see that Ralph daren't look down. The younger boy looked terrified. He tried to step back, but lost his balance and fell.

"No!" the boy with black hair cried out.

"He was called Edmund. He was so frightened," Ralph whispered. "What could I do but try to help him? He was only nine years old. I reached out to comfort him, but I must have alarmed him because he fell. I didn't think, but I leapt after him. I had no thought for myself, and I had no fear. And that's what made the transformation in my blood."

Ralph's eyes burned. "I am more than mortal, a creature outside time and space. I am what Master Burgess would call an angel."

"You fell," Livy whispered. "Like me."

"We jumped, Livy," he said quietly. "To save someone. We didn't think what we were doing and we couldn't know what would happen."

"It's just that Tom is so little." Livy felt as if she was on the verge of tears. "I lost someone before and I couldn't bear to lose Tom."

"But you can't jump if you're frightened, however much powder of alteration you use, however light your blood, because fear is a darker and heavier force than anything that can drag you to the ground. It's like a tiny speck or soot in your heart." He shuddered. "You saw the man. His heart was so dark, the powder made it even darker. He will never walk with angels."

"And you?" Livy asked. "What happens to you?"

"I'm so tired, Livy," he whispered. "I just want it to end."

"That's what my friend Mahalia said," Livy whispered. "The day she gave me her lucky penny." She took it out of her pocket.

"You had a friend that died?" Ralph said, staring at the dull brown coin. "So young."

Livy nodded. "And now she's on her own. I think she's very lonely. Like you."

The boy didn't stiffen as Livy had imagined he might, or move away from her. He smiled sadly, his enormous green eyes looked kind now, not angry.

"I could take it to her," he said gently, lifting it from Livy's palm.

"But how?"

"I would need your help. You know that I am no longer mortal so I cannot die. I have no weight so I cannot fall and time has no effect on me. So I am here, always, endlessly here on the roof of the White Tower." Livy felt his sadness creep across toward her. "All of time is too long to be alone," Ralph whispered. "If you could make me heavy once more, I could cross the barrier to the other realm. That's where your friend is waiting." He held up the coin. "We could share this lucky penny if only you would help me." The blue star above twinkled and Livy had the clearest sense of Mahalia as she had been when she was alive: her mischievous smile, her golden skin, and her thick brown hair.

"Help him." Livy heard that singsong voice whisper to her again. "He's so lonely."

"I need to step back into the mortal world," Ralph whispered. "I need to become heavy as stone and fall through space."

"But that won't work," Livy said. "You won't fall."

"There is a way." The boy looked up at the Sentinel. "My father was the stonemason who carved the Sentinels. After I was changed, Master Burgess was filled with remorse at what he had done to me. He broke the Sentinel's wing." Ralph's eyes clouded. "Will you make him move?"

"Move?" Livy gasped. "But how?"

"Do you remember when you first looked out from your window? What did you see?"

"The sky. The Sentinel."

"But you saw something else. Remember, Livy! Remember how you felt."

Livy took a deep breath and closed her eyes. "I saw the Sentinel; he seemed very close. I reached out and touched him, or so it seemed. And then the stone felt warm to my touch. He seemed to feel my hand and turned his head."

"See? You have made the Sentinel move before," Ralph said. "I saw his wing move and his head turn. And now you must do it again before your blood becomes heavy once more."

"But I don't know how!" Livy protested. "I wouldn't know what to do."

"It's as easy as falling, Livy," Ralph said. "Just allow yourself to do it."

CHAPTER TWENTY-EIGHT

The boy stood up and walked quickly toward the Sentinel. Tom, hunched up in the corner, still did not move.

"We must hurry," Ralph said, holding his hand out to Livy. "This gap between the moments will not last long."

He wrapped his arm around the Sentinel's neck and pressed his dark head to the carved stone breast. Livy reached out and pulled at the thread on Ralph's coat. "I won't forget you," she said.

He put two fingers to his lips and then placed them on Livy's mouth. He was smiling, although Livy felt sure that she could see tears forming. He turned and again put his arm around the neck of the Sentinel. He sighed, as if he were tired, and closed his eyes.

"Ralph," Livy cried out, suddenly panicking. "What happens if the Sentinel doesn't move?"

"Just remember how you warmed the stone."

Livy wanted Ralph to open his eyes again, just so that she could see their remarkable color. "But you can't want this!" she cried out. "I don't believe you."

"But if I stay," he whispered. "I stay forever. And then what will happen when you go? Because you are not like me, Livy. You will not stay as you are. Your blood is not as light and fine as mine, even if you have the power to move the stone and I do not. You will go. You will leave me, as they all do, and I will be even more alone because I will remember what it is like to have someone."

"But . . ."

"Do it now, Livy. In this sliver of nothing between one moment and the next."

Livy took a breath. The air felt heavier. She saw a gust of wind blow Tom's bangs. Was the moment slipping away from her already?

"Quick!" Ralph urged her. "I feel the wind stirring. Time is on the move!"

Livy reached out and touched the stone feathers.

Nothing happened.

She saw Ralph frown, although his eyes remained closed.

"Listen to your blood," he whispered. "Let it move through the stone."

Livy touched the wing once more. Then, when nothing happened, she started hammering her fists on the carved feathers. "Go on! Move!" she yelled up into the unmoving face. "Move! You've got to help me do this for Ralph!"

A tiny pool of rainwater had collected in the corner of the Sentinel's carved eye, although there had been no rain that Livy could remember. It dropped down onto her hands, as heavy as mercury.

She stopped. She looked at the blue star above the Sentinel's head. "I think you have to help me, Mahalia," Livy whispered, on the verge of tears. "I can't do this—I can't send you a friend—on my own."

The star trembled. The Sentinel shivered under Livy's hand and its nostrils flared as if it would breathe. And then it slowly moved its arms to cradle Ralph. The boy tucked his head under the statue's chin.

"One breath more," he whispered to himself. His eyes were still closed as the Sentinel took its first step.

The stone wings were beautiful. "The length of an angel's wing is that of seven celestial kingdoms," Livy whispered, remembering what she had read in the book in the room below. The Sentinel shook them out, and the rush of air was so powerful that it almost threw Livy to the ground. The broken wing quivered and Livy saw how the Sentinel had to try harder to lift it.

"Wait!" Livy cried out as the Sentinel took another long step.

"No," Ralph said. "You must not ask."

"But I want to come with you. I want to see Mahalia again."

"It's not your time, Livy."

The Sentinel moved forward. Livy blinked back her tears. She felt panic rising, overwhelming her. "Tell Mahalia . . ." She reached up and tugged on Ralph's sleeve. "Tell her . . ." It suddenly seemed very important that Ralph tell Mahalia that Livy missed her but that she understood that Mahalia couldn't be with her anymore. *I don't love her any less,* Livy wanted to say, *just because she's gone.*

Ralph smiled, his eyes still closed. "Don't worry," he said. "I'll tell her everything. I'll tell her about you and Tom and that boy who knew I was lost and the girl with the kind eyes. I'll tell her . . ."

And then the Sentinel took another step, and another. It was on the parapet.

"Just one thing more!" Livy cried out, her chest tight.

The Sentinel shuddered.

"Before you go on a journey"—Livy had to get the words out quickly before she began to cry—"you have to say good-bye." She had never been able to say that word to Mahalia. Her throat was very tight now. "So . . . so I won't miss you and wonder where you've gone."

The Sentinel turned its head left and right, seeing the wonder of the vast sky for the first time. Its full lips, carved to look stern and noble, slowly spread into a smile at what its stone eyes could see.

"Good-bye, Livy." Ralph's voice sounded slow and content, as if he was on the edge of sleep.

"Good-bye," Livy said.

The Sentinel folded its heavy carved wings around Ralph and fell forward into the empty, unforgiving air.

CHAPTER TWENTY-NINE

There was a rush of wind, a roar of sound. The tower jolted as if something had slammed into its side.

"That's it, then," Livy whispered.

But, needing to say good-bye one more time and—foolishly, she knew—hoping that Ralph had somehow slipped from beneath the stone wings and was still hanging in the air just below her, she leaned over the parapet. Immediately, her head started spinning. She had to clutch at the stone to stop the tumbling sensation in her stomach.

The Sentinel's head had broken off and had rolled to one side. It stared up at her, a faint look of surprise on its carved features. Its body lay smashed into several large pieces; the wing so large and heavy that the paving stones were cracked around where it had landed. But had it been heavy enough to take Ralph with it? To drag him back into the stream of time and drown him? To make time heavy once more?

And then she saw a single thin plume of smoke rise into the sky and caught that strange metallic scent on the air.

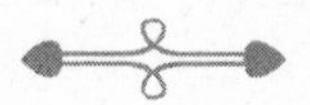

Livy felt a jolt and, as if a movie that had been paused had started again, she saw the trees tremble and wave in the wind. The traffic roared.

"Livy?"

She turned and ran toward Tom and he clung to her tightly. "Count Zacha did not come."

"I'm sorry, Tom," Livy said.

"Will he ever come?"

Livy shook her head. "I think he's gone very far away."

"Like Mahalia?"

"Like Mahalia."

"To the same place?"

"Yes."

"That's good," Tom said. "They can be friends." He hugged Livy tighter. "I am glad Count Zacha didn't come. I don't want to go with him. It is so cold on the roof. The sky is cold." He started to shiver. "He might have taken me a long way away and I might have got lost."

Livy stroked his hair.

"I want to stay with you, Livy."

She kissed the top of his head. "And I want to stay with you."

"Livy? Livy?" They heard Dr. Smythe's feeble voice. "Where are you? Where's Tom? I can't see you. I can't open my eyes."

"Can you come with me, Tom?" Livy asked as she lifted Tom up. "Or do you want to wait here?"

"I can come," Tom said, standing up.

"You must be very careful," Livy said as she climbed over the parapet and onto the roof of the Court of Sentinels. "Don't look down. Then you won't feel dizzy."

"I don't get dizzy." Tom said, swinging his legs over and letting Livy lift him down.

Dr. Smythe raised her head. "Oh, thank goodness," she cried. "You're alive! I thought . . ." She closed her eyes again. "There's a trapdoor just behind us. It's how I got up onto the roof. But I can't move."

"Just sit up," Tom commanded. "Then hold my hand. I am strong, Dr. Smile. And you will not fall!"

Her eyes closed, Dr. Smythe sat up. She clutched her head and then, groaning softly, fell toward the open trapdoor. She disappeared into the square of darkness. Tom scuttled after her. "Be careful!" Livy cried out to him.

Tom turned, his eyes flashing. "I told you! I can fly! I will not fall!"

Tom sat on a large leather sofa in Dr. Smythe's study. He was drawing, lost in concentration. The woman looked out at the dark night. The Sentinel no longer filled the window.

"I felt the ground shake," she whispered. "What happened?"

"It fell," Livy said.

"And Mr. Hopkins?"

"Gone." Livy thought of the pile of dust beneath the Sentinel. "He ran away," she whispered.

"He was not altered?"

"You knew?" Livy gasped.

"All I knew was that he was attempting a dangerous experiment. It's why I fired him. Even though what he was working on would never have actually worked."

"Tom! Livy!" The door burst open and her father stood there, his hair on end. "I've just seen the Sentinel! What happened? Did you see anything?"

Dr. Smythe shook her head.

"Tom! What did I say about not running off in the library? You could have been lost for days!"

Dr. Smythe smiled weakly. "I had my eye on him, James."

Tom looked up from his picture. "Count Zacha didn't

come," he said forlornly. "I waited on the roof with the man. But Count Zacha was busy."

"Well, that's what happens with these superheroes." Livy's father ruffled his son's hair. "They have quite a lot to do. Oh! Livy! You're here! I thought you would have gone home already."

Dr. Smythe spoke again. "When I saw Livy leaving school, I asked her to come and help me look after Tom. I was just about to call you, James, to tell you not to worry. I found him when I was looking for a book in the library."

"I think I found something interesting," Livy's father said as he picked Tom up from the sofa. "A little book on gravity. Mr. Hopkins didn't manage to hide that one from me! I can show you tomorrow."

Dr. Smythe smiled and put her fingers to her temple as if she had a headache. "Just shelve it somewhere," she said quietly. "I'm sorry to have put you to so much trouble, James, but my research has gone in a new direction and I realize that I've no need for that now."

"Livy caught me." Tom sniffed. "When I fell."

"Such an imagination." Dr. Smythe smiled tightly and looked at Livy. "All the while he's been sitting here in my study."

Livy said nothing to contradict her. How could she explain what had happened?

"Perhaps you should take your children home, James. I have work to do. That Sentinel must have been unsafe for a long time. I need to get the maintenance department to make it secure before tomorrow and look into removing the others from the roof." She picked up her phone. "We can't risk an accident."

Livy stepped into the Court of Sentinels; the school was dark and quiet. The only light came from Dr. Smythe's study above, which bathed the fallen statue in a soft golden hue. Tom slipped his hand out of his father's and ran toward the heap of stones.

"Tom!" their father roared. "Stay away from there!"

Tom didn't come back. They ran to catch him and her father snatched him up in his arms.

"His wing didn't work," Tom said sadly, "and so he fell."

Livy's father looked up at the roof, frowning. "It's called gravity, old chap," he muttered, his eyes narrowed thoughtfully.

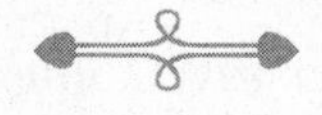

As they turned into Leaden Lane, Livy saw Alex and Celia waiting on the steps of their house.

"We were worried about you," Celia said, her breath coming out in clouds. Livy felt herself blush. What did

they know? What could they have seen? "Your headache," Celia explained.

"Yes!" Livy said. "My headache. All gone now."

"And you said you'd seen Tom on the roof," Celia whispered.

Tom, still in his father's arms, was trying to wink at Alex.

"It must have been a visual aura," Alex said, pleased with himself. "If you have migraines, you often see things that aren't there: flashing lights, zigzags, that sort of thing."

"And brothers?" Celia looked unsure. "You see brothers?"

"I didn't see him," Livy said, looking down. "I was mistaken."

Inside, Livy's mother took Tom from her husband's arms. "You've tired him out, James. All that work!" She smiled at Livy. "You've brought some friends home, Livy. How nice. You haven't done that in a while. Why don't I make some tea and we can crack open the cookie tin!"

"Well, you'd better save some for me!" Livy's father grumbled as he took off his coat. "Mine keep disappearing and I don't even eat them!"

"That happens to me, too!" Livy's mother laughed.

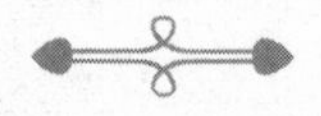

"Did you get my message?" Alex said as they sat around the kitchen table. Livy watched as her father spoke to her mother in hushed tones; she heard the word "Sentinel."

"What?" Livy turned back to look at her friends.

"About the lost boy." Alex was speaking quietly. He glanced over his shoulder at Livy's father. "Don't tell your dad I was in the library. Those records are kept under lock and key. I had to be a little, um, creative to get hold of them."

"Are you two still going on about your lost boy?" Celia hissed.

"But he existed, Celia!" Alex wiped his mouth with the back of his hand.

"What are you three whispering about?" Livy's mother laughed. "I do hope it's a secret! Young people should have plenty of those!"

"Ros!" Livy's father said.

"But it's what friends are for!" Livy's mother sipped her tea. "Keeping secrets."

"Where's my drawing?" Tom said.

Livy's father handed his wife a folded square of paper. Livy's mother smoothed it out and put it on the fridge, securing it with a magnet.

It showed a boy standing on the top of a high tower—Tom, by the look of his messy curls—stepping off into the sky.

CHAPTER THIRTY

There was a group of workmen standing outside the entrance to Temple College the next morning. "How did that thing come down?" Livy heard one of them say. "No storm, nothing."

She walked into the Court of Sentinels. Just six Sentinels on the roof. There were large plastic barriers around the fallen Sentinel and a group of curious pupils were looking at it. Celia waved and called her over. "Mr. Bowen said it will be removed by lunchtime," she chattered excitedly. "They're going to bring a *crane*. But no one can work out how it got here. And how it didn't kill someone!"

They looked down at the Sentinel's face.

"He looks a bit sad," Celia said, serious.

"But peaceful," Alex added.

"Livy?" They turned to see Miss Lockwood,

Dr. Smythe's secretary. "Dr. Smythe would like to see you in her study."

"Will you be OK?" Celia asked, suddenly concerned. "I can wait for you outside."

The window of Dr. Smythe's study looked even emptier in the daylight—no stone wings filled the sky. Dr. Smythe stood up immediately and walked toward Livy.

"How's Tom?" she asked. "After yesterday. Has he said anything?"

"No one really believes him," Livy said. "Whatever he comes out with, my parents just think he's being imaginative."

"He called me Dr. Smile." Dr. Smythe's mouth flickered at the memory. "He's a sweet boy." She bit her lip. "Perhaps it's better if we put down what happened yesterday to our fevered imaginations." She shook her head. "Oh, I put you and Tom in terrible danger, but I had no idea that Mr. Hopkins would attempt such an evil thing. I should have acted sooner. But how could I know that he actually believed what he had ranted to me about?"

She put her hand to her temple. The gold bracelet slipped down her narrow wrist.

"I knew about Master Burgess's work. I knew that he had studied alchemy for many years. But alchemy is not science, Livy. He could not have made gold, as he said he did. He could not have made a child who could fly! Oh, I can see the Sentinels on the roof and the stained-glass window, but I also saw the name of the boy who died. He is mentioned in the school archives. Ralph Symons." She looked away. "What a way to die," she said, her voice no more than breath. "To be pushed from the roof by a man you trusted."

Livy said nothing.

"I think the grief at what he had done to that child unhinged Master Burgess's mind," Dr. Smythe went on. "So he pretended to himself that the boy could fly, and told himself that he had created an angel." She sighed. "And that's where it should have ended. But then Alan Hopkins actually believed the lies that he read in Master Burgess's books. I thought that Mr. Hopkins was weak and vain. I never thought he would be evil enough to try and repeat an ill-fated experiment that had caused the death of that boy so many years ago." She shook her head. "I realized that he was getting into Temple College somehow to carry on with his experiment. I tried to catch him coming in, but he was so sly. But then, when I saw the experiment laid out in the White Tower, I knew that Mr. Hopkins was really crazy. It couldn't possibly work.

He was heating metal filings in a flask! It was the work of a madman . . . So I did nothing to stop it. But he could have caused such harm. Will you forgive me?”

The woman looked anxious still as she looked toward the window “*Tempus fugit.* It did mean something, after all, at least to Alan Hopkins. He thought he could live forever, outside time and space. That his mastery over time meant that he could fly. What a fool!”

What could Livy say? The woman was a scientist, she only believed in what she could see and test through rigorous experimentation. The truth of the matter was in front of her, but she would not, could not, see. “But I am still puzzled—the Sentinel. How did that fall?” She sighed and turned back to face Livy.

“I will be leaving Temple College,” Dr. Smythe continued. “I think this is not the right place for me. I will return to Prague and continue my research into gravity there. But perhaps we can agree to keep this matter between ourselves? No one has been harmed and I have destroyed Peter Burgess’s books. I put them in the fire in that room of the White Tower last night. Let’s hope that I’ve put an end to the matter.”

Dr. Smythe bent down to pick up Tom’s lunch box. “Your brother left this here. Could you return it to him?”

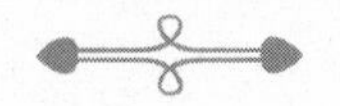

Livy walked slowly down the stairs. *An end to the matter.* Was it over?

She noticed how her blood felt cool and heavy and everything around her seemed as if it was the right weight.

She saw Celia waiting for her at the bottom, her face worried. Livy smiled and waved. "It's all OK," she called down. "Nothing to worry about. Tom left his lunch box in Dr. Smythe's study!"

Celia smiled. Celia. Her friend, Celia. And that was good. It was OK. At last. Mahalia was gone, of course. Ralph, too. And she was sorry. It would always be sad and she wished they could still be here. But they weren't alone anymore. They had each other and Livy felt that Ralph would be a good friend to her. And that Mahalia might bring a smile to Ralph's scowling face after so many centuries of sadness.

Celia put her arm through Livy's. "There's all sorts of stuff going on outside. They're taking the Sentinel away."

Outside, a small crane was positioned next to the broken statue. Workmen were securing ropes around the battered and cracked stone. She watched as the heavy head, carved for Ralph by his father, was lifted slowly into the air.

Her heels stayed on the ground. She didn't want to be on the roof. She could look up at the sky and feel only happiness that she was far below.

She was changed.

Epilogue

"Hey, Joe?"

Livy had run up to the boy in the Court of Sentinels. There were just a few minutes before the start of school. Joe turned in surprise. "That's my name. You're Livy, right?"

Livy nodded. She would have to get this over with quickly if she wasn't going to dissolve on the spot. "Could you do me a favor?"

"It depends . . ."

"I've got a friend—you may have seen me with her."

"She's not one of the deadly duo, is she? The ones that stare and stare and stare . . . Ugh." He shuddered.

"No! Her name is Celia and . . ." Livy stopped for a second. Joe frowned as he waited for her to speak. "She really likes you," Livy blurted out. "But she's not very brave, and so she couldn't tell you herself. But I told her that sometimes you just have to find a way to say these things. So I'm saying it for her. Because she's so shy. I hope you don't mind."

He nodded. He clearly wasn't surprised. "I thought for a moment you were going to say that I owed her money. I borrowed money from a girl last week for some chips and I can't remember who she is so I can't pay her back." He shook his head. "I really hate it when that happens."

"Well! About Celia. You don't have to like her... but..." Joe was smiling now, as if he found Livy amusing. "I had a friend—Mahalia—and she never got to tell this boy that she liked him. I mean, I don't know why she liked him, he looked like a weasel, and had really, really weird hair, but..."

"You can't pick and choose these things," Joe said reasonably.

"Well, that's how Celia feels. My friend. The one I'm telling you about. She's called Celia."

"You told me that."

"Oh. Yeah. Sorry. Well. Could you say hi to her, sometime?"

Joe looked surprised. "Is that it?"

"That's it. Just say hi. Just acknowledge that she's on the earth. And that she's alive. And don't laugh if she can't actually find the courage to say anything back." Livy wanted to kick herself for saying that. It sounded so stupid.

“Sure!” Joe smiled. “I’ll say hi. It’s not a hard thing to do.”

He started to walk away. She had done it.

Joe turned back. “Celia, right? The girl with the black hair and the bangs? She’s in Burgess? Sometimes goes home on my bus. Really, really pretty?”

Livy looked up at the space on top of the White Tower where the Sentinel with the broken wing had once stood. It seemed such a long time ago. It was the time before she could be down here and be happy. It was the time before when Mahalia was still alone. Thinking back to those sad summer days, she knew she would never feel like that again.

She waved discreetly to the empty sky.

ACKNOWLEDGMENTS

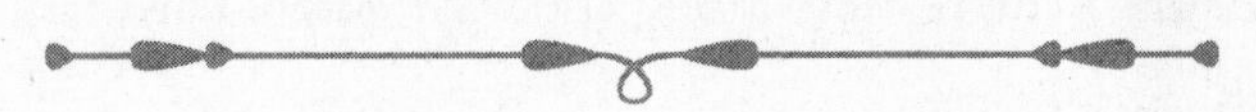

This book has taken far too long to write and I am extremely grateful to many people, mostly for their patience.

Firstly, my wonderful agent, Hilary Delamere, who has given such wise counsel.

Also, my lovely publishers: Barry Cunningham, who didn't blink when he said he liked the book. My editor Rachel Leyshon, who assures me that she still has hair on her head after reading so very many drafts. Rachel Hickman for her calm and enthusiasm in the face of shifting deadlines. Elinor Bagenal, whose energy is infectious. Laura Myers for deftly whizzing through the production. And all the Chickens . . . Jazz, Esther, Kesia, and Sarah. A really lovely team who are passionate about books and the varied imaginative landscapes those books can give to a child.

I'd also like to thank Helen Crawford-White for such an atmospheric UK cover that got the feel of the book even before I'd made the plot any more substantial than smoke.

And for the US edition, I'd like to thank my editor, Nicholas Thomas, the team at Scholastic, and Mélanie Delon and Nina Goffi who designed the cover.

Also to Bella Pearson and Jane Fior, thank you.

And to the readers along the way: Ange, Fatima, and Sarah.

And so, to Charles for pretty much everything; to Milo (for the tours, the music, the general fabulousness); to Rufus who makes me laugh; and to "little" Syrie, raven-haired and six feet tall who has been brave enough to step pretty much anywhere.

Also my sister who has been a peach. And my dear old Dad.

And to mum, twinkling somewhere, love you more.

ABOUT THE AUTHOR

Cathryn Constable is a journalist whose articles have appeared in *Tatler* and the *London Sunday Times*, among other publications. Her debut novel was *The Wolf Princess.* She is married with three children, and lives in London, England.

DISCARDED